D1384871

St. Martin's Paperbacks Titles Featuring Ed and Lorraine Warren

THE HAUNTED
(by Robert Curran with Jack & Janet Smurl
and Ed & Lorraine Warren)

GHOST HUNTERS
(by Ed and Lorraine Warren with
Robert David Chase)

THE DEMONOLOGIST
(by Gerald Brittle)

WEREWOLF
(by Ed and Lorraine Warren with
William Ramsey and Robert David Chase)

GRAVEYARD
(by Ed and Lorraine Warren with
Robert David Chase)

GRAVEYARD

True Hauntings from an Old New England Cemetery

ED AND LORRAINE WARREN

with Robert David Chase

ST. MARTIN'S PAPERBACKS

GRAVEYARD

Copyright © 1992 by Ed and Lorraine Warren with Robert David Chase.

Library of Congress Catalog Card Number: 92-23712

ISBN: 0-312-95113-2

Printed in the United States of America

St. Martin's Press hardcover edition/October 1992
St. Martin's Paperbacks edition/October 1993

10 9 8 7 6 5 4 3 2 1

Names and particulars have been changed in some of the following stories to protect the reputations of both the living and the dead.

In writing this book, I used several sources, including a fine primer entitled *An Introduction to Psychic Studies* by Hal N. Banks, which provided many insights and quotes, and *The Mystic Sciences* by Margaret Waite.

—Robert David Chase

Contents

A quite different phase of Connecticut culture is represented in its graveyards . . . for instance by the huge oblong slabs of rough granite in the graveyard down at Wequetequock, which is part of Stonington. They are called "wolf stones" for the good reason that they were probably intended to prevent wolves of that wild district from disinterring the bodies underneath, and so they lead one's imagination back a long winding way. The largest one, for example, is said to mark the grave of a giant. It is dated 1709.

—ODELL SHEPARD, *Sermons in Stone*

THE STORY
OF UNION
CEMETERY

Introduction

Ed Warren

Many years ago, when Lorraine and I were just starting to investigate supernatural and occult phenomena, we began looking into the history of the state we love so much, and the state we're happy to call home—Connecticut.

You can't be here very long without beginning to sense the fantastic history of the place—fantastic in two respects.

In the Revolutionary War, for instance, Connecticut provided not only strong and willing soldiers but also huge supplies of food, clothing, and armaments. Connecticut played such a key role in supplying American troops, in fact, that George Washington himself called us the Provision State.

Connecticut is fantastic in the other sense, too. From its inception in the early 1600s, when colonists fought the brave and fierce Pequot Indians, our state has been steeped in supernatural and paranormal lore.

Even before Washington and his troops marched, villagers in various settlements reported strange events taking place.

One man reported that his daughter had been "bedeviled" and that, at nine years of age, she was able to stare at an object and "set it afire." Today we call this ability *psychokinesis*.

Not long after this, a woman confided to neighbors that "beings" had taken over her house. The woman constantly heard banging in the walls and bells ringing in the next room and heavy footsteps near her bed at night—yet when she looked, she found nobody. This was obviously an early (and relatively mild) case of poltergeists.

A few decades later, a teenage boy confessed to a Puritan minister that he frequently saw and spoke with the young girl his parents had forbidden him to see—even though the girl had killed herself by drowning two years earlier. The boy was adjudged mad.

Then there were the witches. No region of the United States ever had a period to match early New England's obsession with witches and witchcraft.

A witch is a person who supposedly received magic powers from evil spirits.

In early New England, witches were dreaded for many reasons. It was believed, for example, that a witch could put a curse not only on you or a family member but wipe out your crops or make your cows suddenly go dry. Some midwives swore that they had actually seen witches give birth to monsters. At this time, it was also widely believed that witches rode through the air on brooms. All you had to do was wait till midnight and watch the moon and there, crossing it in silhouette, would be a witch.

Today we consider all this to be sort of silly. While there are indeed evil spirits, and while people do become demonically possessed, the old images of witches don't hold much interest for most people.

Perhaps witches would be a little more frightening to us if we knew how people thought to be witches were treated.

In Europe, witches were tried and executed by the thousands. In certain of the more famous witch trials, children testified against their own parents—then later presided over the execution of those parents. In one case, where an influential man lusted after a certain unobtainable woman, he simply told the court that the woman's husband was a warlock, or male witch. The husband was soon tried and burned at the stake.

Matters weren't much better in New England. People watched their neighbors closely for "devil's marks." These could be anything from a mole that didn't hurt when pricked with a pin to an odd-shaped birthmark. Neighbors actually reported other neighbors as witches with such "evidence."

In one year, 1692, Massachusetts alone executed nineteen people as witches.

In the early 1700s, a new test for witches was devised. If a suspected woman was thrown into the fast currents of the Connecticut river and drowned, then she was most clearly a witch. If she survived—that is, if she knew how to swim—then she was not a witch.

From the very beginning, New Englanders had a fascination with the paranormal.

Gathered around the warm hearth on stormy nights,

New Englanders loved to tell ghost stories, seeing just how much they could scare their friends. The shadows grew long and the fire dwindled to embers before they tired of their ghost stories.

Such famous Puritan ministers as Cotton Mather raged about this fascination, denouncing it as "devil-inspired" and certain to lead to "the greatest loss of all, the loss of one's soul." Mather later played a key role in America's witch trials.

But somehow, despite all the warnings, the people of the New England states never lost the desire to know more about the forbidden and unknown.

With that background, Lorraine and I set out, several decades ago now, to study the state of Connecticut, and in particular the area around Monroe, where we live.

Many people think of our state as a major industrial area, and they're right. We're also known for insurance companies, more than fifty of them headquartered in Hartford alone.

But there's another Connecticut, an older and more venerable Connecticut, a land of covered bridges and Colonial architecture, and small towns. In this older Connecticut, towns have greens, meeting halls, and classic white churches whose spires seem to touch the sky.

This is the Connecticut that Lorraine and I love, especially the town of Monroe.

According to Edward Nicholas Coffey in his fine book *A Glimpse of Old Monroe*, "The town was originally a part of the Stratford Colony and under its jurisdiction for years. It therefore falls heir to Stratford's ancient roots, dating back to its settlement in 1639, less than two decades after the Pilgrim fathers first set foot on New England's coast."

By the time Stratford was settled, the "wolf menace" as it was called, had long been settled.

The Pilgrims wondered if the land was inhabitable because of the wolf packs that roamed the woods destroying large numbers of farm animals.

Though wolves do not frequently attack humans, these wolves constantly stalked the men trying to farm the land.

Coffey wrote: "Even a man was not safe. On one occasion Joseph Curtiss of Stratford led some men to Newton to gather grain. On their way home, passing through this northern area, they were attacked so violently by wolves that they threw down their grain bags and rode their horses home at full speed to spare themselves and their steeds."

In later years, occult investigators wondered about the nature of these wolves—why they behaved so ferociously, and so unlike "normal" wolves.

According to Coffey, early Monroe even had its own sorceress, a "witch" known as Hannah Cranna (though Hovey appeared to be her real last name).

While Coffey didn't put much stock in her supernatural abilities, many of the townspeople did.

They believed that her ramshackle old house was guarded by "snakes of all kinds and all sizes." Few approached her house.

Hannah had no apparent source of income—yet she needn't have worried. The townspeople were so afraid of her curses that they readily gave her food, firewood, and virtually anything else she asked for.

A group of farmers who had angered her found their

crops suffering from drought—and blamed Hannah for cursing them.

A fisherman who usually came home toting several trout found his luck had run out—after Hannah cursed him.

A woman famous for her pies lost her ability to bake well after—you guessed it—Hannah saw fit to curse her.

Hannah had a most curious end.

As Coffey describes it: "On a morning in January after one of the heaviest snows of the winter, a passing neighbor heard a low wail coming from the witch's house. Floundering in the deep snow banks, he waded to the door. The noise subsided and the door opened. There stood Hannah, her face pallid. Inviting him in, she said, 'The spirits have called and it won't be but a short time before I will be in the great beyond. I have a wish to make that must be carried out. I am not to be buried until after sundown and there must be ample bearers to carry my coffin from the house to the grave.'"

She finished by noting, ominously, "Obey my wishes if you would avoid trouble and vexation."

In death she received the same due she'd been paid in life—the townspeople buried her exactly as she'd requested.

Some who rode in the wagon bearing her coffin said that the wooden box shook so fitfully it pitched them to the ground.

After the funeral, Hannah's house inexplicably burned to the ground.

To this day, there are townspeople who insist they can hear moans and howls late at night coming from the site of Hannah's house.

• • •

Today, Monroe is a town of approximately 17,500 people, a bedroom community for the cities of Bridgeport and New York, yet with its own "small town" shopping area, one notable for its distinctively New England aura.

If you drive for very long, you're likely to find a cemetery. One estimate has it that there are more than three thousand marked graves in the township, some of them dating as far back as 1765. In all, there are six cemeteries in the area.

As investigators of psychic phenomena, Lorraine and I have a special interest in graveyards. We know how to listen for—and to—the spirit world. Both Lorraine and I have spoken with the dead on several occasions.

We frequently "visit" graveyards with cameras and tape recorders because sometimes we've been able to get both photographs and audio recordings of spirits.

There are many misimpressions about taking psychic photographs and recordings. For one thing, when most "occult" TV shows look into the matter, they inevitably have the photography taking place at night. Nothing wrong with that—we frequently work at night, too—but it does leave the impression that taking psychic pictures is somehow an eerie business.

It usually isn't.

We take ordinary cameras and ordinary recorders along to the graveyards. No special equipment. And we often work in broad daylight—for a very good reason. It's easier to work with daylight.

When you glance at old gravestones, you often see how lichen and discoloration have given the surface of the stone a mottled appearance. When you look closely at the mottling, you sometimes see patterns, just the way when you stare at clouds sometimes you see patterns or shapes in the sky. Or when you look carefully at ink blots. Well, when you take photographs and develop them, you often see that the "patterns" on the gravestones are really the faces and costumes of the people who are buried there. Over the years, we've learned that spirits project their images on to gravestones and help us take their photographs. Many spirits want to communicate with the living.

This is one form of psychic photography. The other is more haphazard and unpredictable.

In 1893 a California photographer was developing some pictures when he noticed something curious on the negative. The image of the stout society matron he'd been hired to photograph was there, but so was another image, a very faint one of a young and pretty girl. He had no idea who she was.

Curious, the photographer hurriedly developed the rest of his pictures. On each was the image of the matron—and of the young girl.

As it happened, the photographer had dinner that night with some bohemian friends of his, one of whom was interested in the supernatural. She asked if she might see the photographs with the "ghostly" image of the young girl. The photographer was amused. He didn't believe in occult activities but he enjoyed thinking about them.

After looking at the photographs, his friend insisted that the young girl was actually the ghost of a person who had died a violent death in this very building.

The next day, while the photographer spent his time with society matrons who expected him to make them look sleek and attractive, the woman began looking into the history of the photographer's building.

That night, over dinner, she presented him with a curious tale of a fifteen-year-old girl who had been raped and then murdered by her twenty-year-old cousin, a young man who later confessed and was now in prison. The woman had been able to obtain a photograph of the young girl taken shortly before the girl's death. She showed it to the photographer. The girl in his photograph and the girl in the other photograph were the same.

This was one of the first examples of a ghost showing up on a photographic negative.

A few years ago, just to demonstrate that the same thing goes on today, a famous actor divulged on a talk show that when he'd been shooting a motion picture, a woman kept appearing on the finished film—a woman nobody ever saw while the camera was rolling. In other words, a ghost.

And the same is true with audio recordings.

Many times we've taken recorders into a graveyard with us and let the tape roll for hours. We left, thinking that we'd gotten nothing. But at home, when we played the tape back, we heard the voices of the spirits who inhabited the graveyard.

We do most of our investigations with other members of the New England Society for Psychic Research, of which I've been director for many years. The Society meets frequently at the Hawley Manor Inn in New Town.

On a recent talk show, Lorraine was asked by a smirking audience member if the Society was made up of "weirdos."

The lady seemed surprised when Lorraine said, "Not at all. Not unless you consider police officers, clinical psychologists, schoolteachers, and Roman Catholic priests to be 'weirdos.'"

The audience was impressed with Lorraine's response and broke into applause.

Lorraine had certainly been telling the truth. Over the years we've had nearly every kind of professional in our very tight-knit group.

We've even had what I call "professional skeptics" join us, people who don't believe anything unless you can prove it to them several times over, like the schoolteacher I once took into a house infested by demons. Not only did he doubt the existence of demons, he doubted the frantic man who'd called us was even telling the truth. "He just wants some publicity," my skeptical Society friend said.

Well, he remained skeptical right up to the moment when dishes and glasses and silverware began flying through the air in the kitchen, nearly cutting off one of his ears in the process. He ran out the back door and straight back to our car, locking himself inside.

From doctors to housewives, the Society has attracted many different types of people over the years.

And it was members of the Society who first began hearing rumors about Union Cemetery.

As Lorraine and I mention in our lectures, New England graveyards are frequently "haunted" in the sense that we've encountered many spirits in them.

Oddly, we'd never paid much attention to Union Cemetery, which is only a few minutes away from our home in Monroe.

Union Cemetery is a beautiful, rolling site with a rural highway running right alongside it. While we'd passed by it many times over the years, we had never looked into its history.

Several members of the Society, however, started writing down all the stories they heard about the cemetery, and very soon nearly everybody in the Society was involved in looking into Union's history.

Now we're glad we spent all those days and nights working on the cemetery project. It certainly yielded many new insights into the paranormal and gave us even more proof that most graveyards are fascinating studies unto themselves . . . especially if you're interested in the supernatural.

Lorraine Warren

All the stories you've heard about New England in the fall are true. It is the most beautiful countryside I've ever seen, especially the flowers such as white woodland aster, boneset, and the heath aster when they're in bloom. The hills are smoky and melancholy in the warm fall sunlight, and bright with the fiery leaves of trees such as poplar and beech and ash and maple.

During the autumn months you get a real sense of history, especially when you contemplate the lost Indian trails that wind through the deep, brilliant forests.

One of my favorite books on the state is Odell Shepard's classic *Connecticut, Past and Present,* in which he says:

"One must try to remember that the first white settlers came here precisely to get away from trees. The forest to them was the enemy, to be conquered by any means fair or foul. To those first-comers chipping away with their bog-iron axes it must have seemed almost invincible, inexhaustible; and yet, seeing it as the lurking-place of wild beasts, wild men, and the Devil's cohorts, they felt that it must be overcome if they themselves were not to be pushed back into the sea. . . . From the forest, a little later, they carved their farms and cut their roads. Out of the forest came their food and furniture, their cradles and coffins."

And, as Odell points out in the same book, these same people became fascinated with gravestones and cemeteries:

"The once common assertion that the Puritans of New England had no sense of beauty looks absurd, of course, in the light of what we know today about their churches, houses, furniture and even their rough-hewn music; but the most emphatic refutation of the charge has not yet been made. It is to be found in the work of the stone-cutters who carved the emblematic figures inscribed on nearly every headstone set up in New England in her first two centuries."

The Society shares Odell's interest in graveyards. Along with their aesthetic appeal—the sloping hills and iron fences and the white stone monuments ablaze in the autumnal sunlight—cemeteries offer people like us a glimpse of New England's occult history as well.

One of our members learned this, several months after first telling us about Union Cemetery, when he received a phone call telling him about two brothers who were willing to discuss seeing the famous "White Lady" so many locals had heard of since they were children.

This was his first real lead in unraveling the story of Union Cemetery.

Soon after this, Ed and I began hearing stories about several tragic events that had happened to people who lived in and around the cemetery.

Over the coming months the Society started to see how much Union Cemetery resembled the "negative aspects of the ground" we'd found in other parts of the world—a section of country where tragedy takes place at a rate that would defy statistical probability.

We now believe that Union Cemetery has long exerted a dark influence on the lives of many people living within a six-mile radius of it.

A Case of
Lust and Murder

THE PURITANS had a particular horror of adultery. To them it was one of the most serious sins because it threatened the sacredness of the family.

In the legend and lore of New England the consequences of adultery abound. In New Hampshire, for example, it is told that a wife who was unfaithful was beheaded by her husband—and now the woman roams the deep woods at night in a fine white gown covered with blood. And minus her head. This particular sighting has been reported since the early 1800s.

In another incident, this one taking place in Maine, a man and woman met frequently in a wooded glen. Both were married to other people. Both were satisfied to keep their affair going for as long as possible. One night in the glen, just as the couple was starting to make love, a strange young man appeared and stood but a few feet behind where they lay in the grass. The woman then heard a wailing that forced them apart, the saddest sound that had ever touched her ears. She pushed her lover away and went to the strange young man who stood on the edge of the glen. He continued his crying, obviously deeply aggrieved. Her lover neither saw nor heard the young man. He was probably wondering if the woman had suffered some kind of breakdown.

In the moonlight, there in the glen, the woman put her hand out to touch the young man's shoulder but found that her hand went right through him. He was not of this earth, the young man. She started to turn and call out for her lover but he had taken off for home, running. The woman was behaving insanely; she would get them both in trouble.

The woman, too, wanted to leave but something held her here. She realized that she was totally alone in the deepest woods at the darkest hour. The young man before her was now shimmering, like a ghostly picture flickering in and out of sight. Only his cry remained steady and true.

And then he spoke to her. Not in words. In pictures . . . pictures that he somehow projected into her mind. She saw a young, happy family—vibrant young wife, two nice children, and a husband . . . the same young man standing next to her tonight.

And then the pictures changed. She saw the vibrant young wife in the arms of another man, about to make love. And then a picture of the young husband throwing himself off a stone bridge late one frosty February night, breaking through the ice and sinking deep into the cold, dark water where, a few minutes later, he drowned.

And now, forever roaming these woods where his wife had betrayed him, the spirit of this man wept for the life that had once been his before his young wife's adultery destroyed it.

Chastened, knowing there was no way that she could console this spirit, the woman went home and was never again unfaithful, now that she understood how destructive the effects of adultery could be.

In the files of Union Cemetery there's a tale that involves adultery—of sorts. It should probably be called failed adultery because it concerns a man who lusted after another man's wife and in so doing destroyed three lives, including his own.

That particular autumn, several decades ago, was notable for its summerlike warmth. The warm days stretched all the way into November.

The woman's name was Ellen and she was most attractive. At the church where she was the organist, it was not uncommon for young men to develop intense crushes on her.

Unfortunately for her would-be suitors, Ellen was happily married to a man named John Smathers, a workman who spent his days at a nearby plant, and his weekends tramping across the countryside. He loved the outdoors.

At this time a man named Richard Jason also lived near Monroe and frequently saw the Smathers woman as she walked about the town. She often walked past Union Cemetery, especially on pleasant days. Dogs and kittens invariably followed her. They seemed as much taken with her as all her would-be suitors.

Jason was something of a mystery man. He'd only been in the area for a few months, he didn't have any sort of job, and yet he seemed to live reasonably well, renting a small apartment in a gracious old boarding house and spending a lot of time ingratiating himself with the older citizens, whom he saw during the daytime when everybody else his age was off working or home with the children.

Though the story of his carnival life was never authenticated, it was rumored that Jason had spent his younger years as a carny who worked for a mentalist with the unlikely name of Swami Lorenz. One spring, the story went, Swami Lorenz gazed into his crystal ball and saw something that genuinely disturbed him. He saw Jason take the voluptuous Narda, the trapeze artist, into the Tunnel of Love and there try to choke her because he'd learned she'd been unfaithful. He warned young Jason not to take Narda into the Tunnel, but Jason did so anyway. And there in the darkness, in the row boat that went around the track through the water, Jason found himself possessed by a rage he'd never known. He accused Narda of betraying him, and he was choking her when Swami Lorenz caught up with them and saved the young woman. Disgraced, Jason fled the carnival and spent several years drifting around the country until he came to the area of Union Cemetery.

That autumn Richard Jason became obsessed with Ellen Smathers. He followed her everywhere, he frequently tried to get her to go places with him, he phoned her whenever her husband was away.

People who knew him at this time said that he seemed to go literally insane over her.

Two or three times he snapped photographs of her and apparently carried them with him wherever he went. He'd stop and stare at them and then go looking for her, the way "stalkers" sometimes operate today.

His landlady later told the police of a curious incident that happened one stormy night shortly after Jason moved into the boarding house. She was fixing her late-night tea when she heard a sudden ruckus above her in Jason's apartment. She went up to find out what was going on. When he came to the door, she saw that the floor was strewn with cups and saucers and plates that had been smashed to the floor.

But that wasn't all—directly behind him was a plate that was not only suspended in midair but was slowly moving across Jason's room.

The landlady, a regular reader of *Fate* magazine, knew all about poltergeist activity. She knew that while most such activity tends to center around children, there were also cases where very troubled adult minds—minds that could be called psychotic—also generated such incredible poltergeist phenomena.

And obviously, that's what was going on here!

For a few days following this incident, the landlady tried to sneak into Jason's apartment and see if he had any occult paraphernalia. But Jason, contrary to house rules, had padlocked his room. And she was afraid to ask him for a key.

Day in, day out, Jason followed the Smathers woman. He earnestly believed that one day he would possess her in all senses of that word. She would not merely leave her husband willingly. She would give herself to Jason completely: he would rule her utterly. And she would love it!

Eventually, John Smathers became aware that Richard Jason was stalking his wife.

In fact, some townspeople insist that John even paid Jason a visit on a few occasions, angrily warning Jason to stay away from her.

Then the fantasy that so consumed Jason—that Ellen

would someday be his bride—took a new and even more dangerous turn.

Jason became convinced—and this clearly points up his insanity—that if John Smathers were to die, Ellen would then marry him.

Over the next month Richard Jason made his plans.

He would murder John Smathers and bury the body in a sinkhole not far from the cemetery, behind the Baptist church. He would weight the body down and put it so deep into the sinkhole that nobody would ever see it again.

For nearly a week Ellen was left alone. Assuming that Jason had finally given up, she spent a very peaceful and happy week in her house.

Then John failed to come home one night after work. He sometimes had to work overtime, and at first she thought he would phone to tell her where he was and when he'd be home.

Midnight came and went. She began to panic. John was the most reliable of husbands. No matter what happened, he always called.

In the morning Ellen Smathers called the police. They ascertained that John had gotten off work at the regular time and had started to come straight home. Somewhere along his usual route, however, he was waylaid and disappeared.

As he would later recall it, Richard Jason was standing at the sink, shaving, and watching the arc of his safety razor in the mirror—when he felt the bathroom temperature drop at least ten degrees. At first he thought that a window might have eased open, but there were no windows in the bathroom.

And then a terrible stench—all he could think of was

the hog kill on a hot day back in the small town where he'd been raised—filled the room.

He realized, abruptly, that someone stood behind him. His eyes momentarily left the mirror, and when they returned, they saw a dark man-shape in the glass.

Jason froze. He wanted to scream. He felt as helpless as a six-year-old.

And then the shape moved across the bathroom to the wall. It hesitated—and then walked directly into the wall and vanished.

Jason left the shaving cream on his face and quickly retreated to his room where he sat on the edge of the bed, reliving last night. Following John Smathers to his car . . . knocking him unconscious . . . bludgeoning his head with a hammer . . . and then taking him to the sinkhole, tying weights to him and pushing him so far down that he would never be seen again.

Everything would be all right, Jason had reasoned all last night. Eventually Ellen would come to believe that her husband had deserted her, and she would turn for comfort and solace to the man who had loved her so long. . . .

Jason sat in his room, trembling still because of the sudden drop in temperature.

He kept trying to convince himself that what he'd seen in the bathroom had been nothing more than a hallucination. He was tired, nervous, imagining things.

And then, hearing the boards of the hardwood floor squeak, he looked up and saw next to the bureau the dark man-shape emerge from the wall again.

Jason ran to the door, ripped it open, hollered for his landlady to come up here fast!

He knew how embarrassing it was for a grown man to sound hysterical this way but—

"In my room," he said when the landlady reached the second floor. "There's something in there!"

She gave him a most peculiar look, shook her head, and went into the room.

In her time the landlady had seen many men suffer from delirium tremens. Drinking to excess inhibits the dreaming process and so, unable to dream while sleeping, alcoholics start dreaming while they're awake. Or having nightmares.

And that's what she believed this was. Jason had a fondness for booze, anyway. Between not sleeping much and drinking too much, a man was bound to start getting spooked.

She searched sleeping room and bathroom and found, as she'd expected, nothing untoward.

By this time, several of her other boarders had gathered in the hall to see what was going on. They all stared knowingly at Jason. They disliked and distrusted him, and weren't at all surprised to find that he was having some kind of breakdown.

The landlady came out and pronounced the room safe. She did this with a wink and a smirk to her other boarders.

Frightened, Jason inched his way back into his room.

As soon as he closed the door, the other boarders broke into a laugh.

Stupid sonofabitch. Serve him right for drinking the way he did.

That night, Jason slept with the light on. Like a child.

He had dreams of this strange dark man-shape chasing him down an endless, narrow alley lit only by occasional torches. The ground writhed with hundreds of thick black snakes. He knew that if he fell, they would envelop him and—

He woke up screaming.

At first, he had no idea who he was.

And then he remembered.

And remembered what he'd done.

Smathers. Dead. Sinkhole.

But nobody would ever find him.

Ever. Not with the iron weights Jason had tied to the body.

Not with the sinkhole that deep.

No. Nobody would ever find him. . . .

For the next few days, search parties of men and dogs went throughout the countryside, trying to find a body. None was found.

One policeman reported having a dream in which he saw John Smathers falling down a vortex of some kind. The dream made no sense and was discounted by everyone, including Ellen Smathers.

Richard Jason drove around and watched it all, the packs of men, the packs of dogs.

He ate well. He slept well. He sat in his room at night listening to the traffic, sipping on a bourbon and water, making his plans for the proper time.

He wasn't sure when that would be, when it would be seemly for him to walk up to Ellen's door and ask her if he might come inside, and sit on her couch and hand over a bouquet of fresh-cut flowers and. . . .

Months, probably, before it would be the proper time.

Because otherwise people would talk.

Because otherwise people would suspect.

Because otherwise the police might think. . . .

Several more days passed.

Richard Jason saw Ellen on the sunny street one day and he was shocked.

Her eyes were sunken and dark, she had dropped at least ten pounds, and she was no longer the fastidious dresser she'd once been. She looked rumpled and even, despite her beauty, dowdy.

How could she have let herself go this way?

When he started courting her, he would convince her to start dressing well again.

Eventually, the police gave up their search. John Smathers was nowhere to be found.

People began returning to their normal lives. Oh, the exact nature of the crime was still speculated on over coffee, and little kids still dreamed of the bogeyman hiding in their shadowy closets, but John Smathers was just plain gone.

Several times a day, Richard Jason drove by the white church with the sinkhole behind it.

Down in that sinkhole was the body of John Smathers. Jason felt no remorse for his crime. In fact, he felt a kind of perverse pride. He'd weighted the body down by sticking five pound pieces of iron in all the pockets.

Smathers was gone for good.

Jason had just gone to sleep when he heard the shouting down the street.

At first he thought he might be having a nightmare.

It was late . . . time for sleep . . . who would be shouting now?

He got up and went to the window and pulled back the drapes and looked out.

The midnight street was dark in the early autumn

night. At the corner a lone street light revealed a small group of men piling into the back of a pick-up truck.

These were the men who were shouting.

What was going on?

Richard Jason felt a paralyzing panic. All he could do for several long minutes was stand in the middle of his room in his underwear and make the kind of angry, whimpering noises that animals make when they're frustrated.

Somehow he knew that the body had been discovered.

But how?

He'd weighted the body down . . . pushed it deep into the sinkhole . . . left no trace of blood or clothing.

How could the body have been discovered?

Jason couldn't resist going to the church to make sure.

By the time he got there, he found the church grounds lit up. There must have been twenty men, including the police, encircling the sinkhole.

He stood on the road, watching.

"He floated right to the top," a man said. He'd come over to ask Jason for a match. "Had weights tied to him and everything, but he floated right to the top, anyway. Just like he wanted to make sure that we knew he was down there. Ain't that strange?"

The man from the medical examiner's office knelt next to the dead body sprawled on the lawn of the church. "Never seen anything like it. Like the earth just spit him back up or something . . . like somebody wanted us to find him."

"All those weights," said an onlooker. "How could he ever come back to the surface like that?"

The medical examiner's man shook his head. "Isn't

likely we'll ever know. Not the sort of thing anybody can ever find an answer to. It . . . just happened, I guess."

Five minutes later, Jason was back in his room. But he wasn't sleeping. He was packing, flinging all his clothes into two large suitcases.

Time to go.

Time to get as far away from here as possible.

He packed in the dark. The only light came from the distant streetlamp. He was covered with an icy sweat.

He was just reaching the doorknob when he heard them.

Two sets of footsteps on the stairs.

Coming up.

Coming straight for his room.

He looked frantically at the window.

Would there be time to open it up and—

"Mr. Jason," said a man's voice. "This is the chief of police and I'd like to talk to you a minute."

Jason dropped his bags and tiptoed to the window.

He was just sliding up the bottom half, just smelling the cold crisp air of this October night when the door opened and there—large revolver in hand—stood the chief of police.

The chief was almost as big as the doorway itself.

"I think it's time I take you down to the station and we have ourselves a little talk, Mr. Jason."

By dawn Richard Dean Jason had confessed to the murder of John Smathers. He was promptly put in jail, the judge imposing an extremely high bail.

During his life in prison, two things occupied Jason's mind.

He wondered why Ellen Smathers never answered any of the letters he dutifully sent her each month.

And he wondered how a weighted-down body had ever floated to the top of a sinkhole.

It was almost as if unseen forces had helped push the body up. . . .

Richard Dean Jason spent the rest of his life in prison.

While the story about Jason's visit from the dark man-shape has never been verified, several prisoners swore that Jason confided it to them over the years of his confinement . . . still searching, apparently, for some explanation as to how a heavily weighted-down body could rise to the surface of a sinkhole.

The Lonely Sexton

A FEW MONTHS ago the host of a TV show devoted to the occult used the terms *ghost* and *apparition* as if they meant the same thing. They don't. Generally, ghosts are "dumb"—they stay in the last place they occupied on earth, they rarely communicate, and they are only occasionally malicious. Essentially they are beings that have not resolved all their earthly sorrows and so now wander about hoping to do so.

Apparitions are a far different matter. For one thing, they often interact with their earthly hosts. For another, they frequently have the power to warn earthly friends of dire consequences about to befall them.

A famous rock star has told the story about boarding a touring bus one night—and then getting back off it before he even reached the back seat.

Standing in the aisle, near the back, was the apparition of his cousin, a boy he'd grown up with but a boy who, sadly, had been killed in a farming accident when he was fourteen years old.

The cousin now warned the rock star that something terrible was going to happen aboard the bus that night.

The rock star, shaken, stood there looking right at his cousin, who looked just the same as he had the night before his death. Only when headlights washed across the bus window did the rock star see that his cousin was not really flesh and blood but rather a kind of motion picture projection.

The rock star was so alarmed by what he saw that he got off the bus immediately, walked down the street, rented a car and drove himself to the next day's gig. Three hours later, the bus was involved in an accident that killed the driver and a passenger.

Another famous story about apparitions involves the hangman who was visited the night before an 1883 execution by the man he was to hang in the morning.

The man protested his innocence and said there would be dire consequences for the hangman if he went through with the execution.

The hangman's wife sat up in bed and wondered who her husband was talking to in the darkness. She could not see his visitor.

In the morning the execution went off on schedule. The prisoner's neck was broken at once.

For the next month the hangman stayed around home. The apparition had frightened him. His wife noticed that for the first time in his life, her husband went around talking to himself.

A few nights later she woke up in the middle of the night to find her husband gone. Afraid, she found her kerosene lantern, got it lighted, and went through the house in search of her husband.

She found him in the basement. He had wrapped a rope around a beam, tied the rope into a noose, and hanged himself.

She ran from the house, shrieking.

A neighbor came back and cut her husband down. But by then he was already dead.

Upstairs, she found a note: "*I did not hang myself. Bryce Holland hanged me.*"

Nobody could ever understand what he meant by this note. Bryce Holland was the name of the prisoner the hangman had executed a month earlier.

The Union Cemetery files has its own story of apparition and obsession. . . .

Most people had a difficult time knowing what to make of forty-one-year-old Don Parrish. A gifted architect who had survived an ordeal with cancer, Don should have been a family man and a real part of his community.

Instead, he spent his spare hours acting as the sexton of the cemetery, making certain that vandals hadn't done any damage to the headstones, helping tend the grounds, sometimes even doing handywork for hours on end.

Don also loved to hike. He told his few friends that nothing made him happier than taking his skis and going to the Adirondacks to fish and hunt in bitter winter. He obviously appreciated the white beauty of the mountains.

And when Don didn't have time to travel, he put on his snowshoes and tramped around the countryside near the cemetery.

He was doing this the day he saw the person he would later describe as "the dark man."

The sun was shining. There were western winds that kept the snow blowing in golden clouds, half-blinding Don as he tromped across the hills on his cross-country skis.

He was just coming down the slope leading to the cemetery, when he saw a man dressed in the black clothes of a minister . . . but a minister from two centuries earlier.

"Hello!" Don called above the wind. But the minister didn't seem to hear. He just kept walking up the hill.

Don moved quickly, trying to catch the man and talk to him.

He just kept wondering: why would somebody dress up this way and walk across the hills, especially three days before Christmas when it's this cold?

But he didn't catch the man. The elusive black-clad figure wove in and out of the whirling snow.

Don just watched as the dark figure approached the crest of the hill—and then vanished.

There was no other way to say it. The dark man had been there—and then the dark man was gone.

Simply gone.

Over the course of the next few weeks, Don lost interest in everything except the dark figure he'd seen on that sunny winter afternoon.

He finally confided what he'd seen to his friend Aaron. He even convinced Aaron to go up in the hills around the cemetery and look for the dark man.

Don and Aaron spent most of their free time searching for the dark man.

But the search was useless.

They saw nothing.

Aaron obviously began to wonder if Don hadn't hallucinated, if the dark man wasn't a creation of Don troubled mind. The bout with cancer had cost Don a lot of energy . . . and maybe in a weakened state . . . well, maybe Don was simply imagining things.

But after one late Friday afternoon jaunt through the hills, all Aaron's doubts were taken away.

They were just heading back to the cemetery, frustrated as usual by not seeing anything, when Don said, "Look!"

At first, Aaron's mind refused to believe what his eyes saw.

Twenty yards away from the perimeter of the cemetery stood a young man in the deerskins and raccoon hat of a seventeenth-century deerstalker. The skins were grimy and well-used. He looked as shocked by them as they were by him. He kept staring at their clothes.

"Where are you going?" Don asked.

And when the young man spoke, it was in a tongue that bore only a slight resemblance to the English language of today.

He said he planned to meet some friends of his by cutting across the field here.

Don recognized immediately that something was very wrong here.

First of all, the "friends" the young man had mentioned were familiar to Don. But he wasn't quite sure why. . . .

Second of all, the path the young man proposed to take was impossible because it would lead him directly through the Easton Reservoir. A man who'd been born a century ago wouldn't know about the reservoir. . . .

The young man started to walk away.

Don and Aaron called for him to wait.

But, just as with the dark figure, the young man

vanished before they could stop him and ask him more questions.

Don had always been interested in the history of the region. He had a considerable library of books devoted to the legends and lore of the area.

He also had a book that listed the names of the early settlers.

Among those names, Don found the people the young deerstalker had spoken of as his friends.

No wonder the names had sounded vaguely familiar to Don. They were names he'd come across in his history books many times.

Which meant that the young man they'd seen had had to be at least—two hundred years old!

Aaron accepted the truth. He became interested in paranormal matters. He would spend his life deeply intrigued by the occult and the supernatural.

Don didn't respond nearly as well.

His encounter with the spirit of the deerstalker disturbed him.

He had trouble sleeping. He lost considerable weight. He had no energy.

Friends of his mention that he began to delve into the nature of ghosts and learned that, as TV producer Alan Landsburg said in his book *In Search of . . .* , "A ghost is a split-off personality that remains behind in the environment of the person's previous existence, whether home or place of work, but closely tied to the spot where the person actually died. Ghosts do not travel, do not follow people around, and they rarely leave the immediate vicinity of their tragedy."

Or, as Margaret Waite in her book *The Mystic Science*

noted, famed occult writer Hans Holzer "believes that all ghosts are psychotic, disoriented entities that have been unable to rise above some massive tragedy in his physical life.

"Holzer propounds an interesting theory that man's emotional tensions might constitute an electromagnetic field similar to a radiation field in the atmosphere. 'After all,' he asks, 'if an atomic explosion can make a part of the atmosphere radioactive for many years, why not a miniature outburst such as sudden death?'"

This kind of "atmosphere" might explain Don's slip into deep depression. He saw something symbolic—and something of himself—in the mysterious deerstalker who plied the same area year after year, era after era.

Don began to weaken noticeably. Now he spent many hours sleeping, and he cut off communications with several of his friends.

He could sometimes be seen staring at the hill where he'd first glimpsed the mysterious deerstalker.

His doctor was concerned that the cancer had returned but test after test showed that Don had no physical troubles.

Some believe that, during this time, Don was visited by a "discarnate," a spirit whose earthly personality has survived death completely. Unlike a ghost, which rarely communicates, or a spirit, which often communicates but is usually single-minded, focusing on warnings for the earthbound—unlike these, a discarnate is a "full-bodied" spirit, so to speak, capable of expressing most human emotions . . . pleasure, pain, sadness, even jealousy. In the 1930s, popular fiction was filled with tales of lonely young men who fell in love with beautiful female discarnates. Thorne Smith, creator of Topper, wrote several such novels.

The discarnate who may have visited Don was prob-ably brought in through the portal of Don's own interest in the occult . . . and his own anxiety about his death. His cancer was never far from his mind.

Some say that the discarnate who contacted him was generous of heart and spent her time with Don reassur-ing him that there was a much better world beyond this life.

Whatever was on his mind, Don decided to find out about the "better world" for himself.

A few weeks later, he committed suicide.

On the day Don was buried, a local conservation officer reported seeing the mysterious figure of a man dressed in deerstalker clothes standing on the hill above the graveyard.

Watching.

The Haunted Monastery

ACCORDING TO occult theory some of a body's energy remains in it after death, so a fresh corpse was required [for the sacrifice]. It was taken to a dark place screened by yews, cut open and annointed with a mixture of warm menstrual blood, the froth of rabid dogs, the hump of a corpse-fed hyena, the sloughed skin of a snake and the leaves of a plant on which Erictho had spat," wrote Margaret Waite in her book *The Mystic Sciences*.

Her description is of an early Roman attempt to practice necromancy, which means, essentially, to draw up the spirits of the dead and to enlist them in helping you commit great sins or crimes.

Necromancy may seem irrelevant to a century as "wise" as ours, but a glance at some of our serial killers shows otherwise. Both Charles Manson and Ted Bundy expressed interest in the occult, specifically necromancy.

And with the rise of satanic cults in America today, necromancy is being practiced once again.

The New England Society for Psychic Research is frequently called in to investigate graveyards where necromantic activity has been going on. As Ed Warren noted on a talk show recently, "Some people read a book on black magic and then rush to the nearest graveyard to raise up dark spirits. Because nothing happens right away, these people feel they've failed and go on to something else. Unfortunately, the supernatural world doesn't work that way. When you summon demons and spirits, they usually come, even if it takes awhile. We've picked up a lot of demonic activity in graveyards lately, and it's usually the result of all these would-be necromancers."

In the annals of Union Cemetery, necromancy can be found in the strange case of the Haunted Monastery.

Several decades ago a group of devout monks came to the area to build a monastery. It would be a fine and noble monument to God, as they saw it, incorporating native stone and timber, and rising high on a hill to commune with the stars in the vast New England night.

History tells us that in the Dark Ages there were some monasteries, in the hinterlands of Europe, that gave themselves over to doing Satan's work.

Many a priest, seeking shelter from a fierce storm, found himself sitting across a bare wood table in a dungeonlike room from a monk whose dark eyes reflected the madness of his pact with Satan.

These renegade monks were necromancers, and woe betide the traveler who fell into their hands. One such holy priest later told of witnessing a midnight ceremony in a subbasement wherein a fifteen-year-old virgin girl from the nearby village was first raped and then cut apart with long knives that glowed in the candlelight. She would be used as a sacrifice to call up the dead. The priest escaped, fleeing to Paris where he warned the great archbishop himself of this vile sect. The archbishop dispatched three of his best warrior-priests to deal with these infidels. But when the priests arrived, they found the monastery empty and the monks long gone.

In the ensuing years the archbishop decided that the monastery should be reconsecrated and used by the Dominican friars. But after several different groups of friars and monks tried living there, the archbishop came to the conclusion that the land on which the monastery had been built was uninhabitable. No crops would grow there; the well water was so bitter as to be un-drinkable; and from the ground itself came the screams and moans of the demonic dead.

The ground was accursed and therefore useless to all who honored the ways of the Lord.

At the monastery in the region of Union Cemetery, nothing went right. No matter how long and carefully the monks worked on the foundation, it was never quite right. No matter how hard they worked on construct-ing the roof, the frame kept collapsing. And there were fires, inexplicable flames flickering up from nowhere and destroying much of the work that had already been done there.

Today, when you walk up the hill to the monastery, you see that all that remains are a few stones and some rubble. You can see where the foundation had been planned, and how the windows would have allowed the monks to stare up at the stars at night, and where a large garden was to have grown.

But today all that remains is a few stones and some rubble. You stand on the hill and hear the long sighing of the wind and see how grass and weeds have overgrown all the hard work the monks gave to this place.

You get the same sense standing in the ruins of an Inca temple . . . of a majestic past overtaken by time and the whim of the dark gods.

The Society spent a long spring investigating the land on which the monastery was to be built.

It is the Society's opinion that the land is accursed.

In the late 1800s a group of people traveled through this area and stayed for nearly a month, living in primitive conditions. There was trouble with some townspeople and trouble with the law. There were also rumors of strange activities at night. After the people had left, the clean bones of many dead animals were found in a sandy pit, and several satanic symbols were later discovered carved into many trees. Many of these people camped where the monastery was eventually to be built.

While today there is no record of these people having been here—rumor and gossip sometimes invent such "people"—the Society feels that they did exist, they did stop here, and they did perform necromantic rites on the land . . . and thus it became accursed ground.

The building stands today . . . its majesty lost to the long grasses and weeds. When you go there, as Ed and I did recently, you are reminded of what it's like to walk among the ruins of a vanished civilization.

The land is still used for satanic activities.

On a recent field trip, Society members passed by the old monastery grounds and found black candles and other black magic paraphernalia. Satanists have apparently drifted back to the old site, and are using it again.

No wonder the holy monks gave up on their monastery . . . and fled the accursed ground.

The Burning Man

THE SUBJECT of demonic possession continues to fascinate most people. Network TV abounds with shows devoted to demonic possession, and every few years a book devoted to possession becomes a best-seller.

As an example, Ed and Lorraine Warren became involved in a famous Connecticut murder trial in which a young man was accused of murder.

As Ed told the story in *Ghost Hunters*:

Q: How did you get involved in the case?

Ed: Very simply. Lorraine and I were sitting at home one Sunday night and the phone rang. We were told that an eleven-year-old boy was suffering a demonic attack.

Q: Did you go right to the scene?

Ed: No. Over the years we've learned that many so-called supernatural events are really just people suffering breakdowns of various sorts. They hallucinate, they hear things, and people around them begin to think that they're seeing something from another realm.

Q: What did you see when you checked out eleven-year-old David Glatzel?

Ed: Well, we ended up going over there and brought an M.D. along. You see, there was sort of a wild card with David Glatzel. He suffered from a learning disability. We knew this physician whose son suffered from the same problem, so we asked him to go along and interpret what we saw. We didn't want to confuse something that stemmed from being learning disabled with the supernatural. That's why we take doctors and psychotherapists and priests and police officers along whenever possible. That way we ensure that we're getting the situation evaluated from at least two very different perspectives.

Q: Did it turn out to be an exciting night?

Ed: Yes. David told us that earlier in the day he'd gotten tired and lain down. While he was in bed, an old man appeared to him. The old man was dressed in a plaid shirt and jeans with a rip in the right knee, and he looked straight at David and said "Beware." Then later in the day, after David had told his mother about the old man, the boy lies down again and there's the old man in the room once more. Only this time, instead of feet, the old man has hooves and his body looks charred now, as if he survived a terrible fire. These are classic symbols of demonic infestation.

Q: Where did the case go from here?

Ed: Well, we stayed in touch with the boy and his parents. David continued to have periodic "break-downs" in which he saw spirits and demons. And he would speak in voices that weren't his own.

Q: And then what?

Ed: Well, David grew up and became very good friends with a boy named Arnie. Arnie was engaged to David's sister. Arnie was so worried about David and his demons that one night, when David was having an especially bad infestation, Arnie started shouting at the demons to attack him and leave David alone.

Q: And did they attack him?

Ed: Not only attacked him but completely took him over.

Q: How so?

Ed: Arnie was a very decent kid. Didn't hurt people. Was reliable in every respect. Yet, next day at the place where he worked, he took a knife and stabbed his boss to death. Totally out of character. Totally inexplicable. He was tried for murder, of course.

Q: You tried to help him?

Ed: Yes. We tried to get the court to understand that Arnie had been demonically possessed. That it was not really him doing the attacking.

Q: He went to prison?

Ed: Yes, he did but he's out now and leading a decent life.

In 1935, America was still deep in the Depression. Nightly radio news and weekly newsreels at movie theaters showed a country in tragic condition—soup lines, men hurling rocks through the windows of closed factories, men standing on the curb holding signs: "My Child Needs Food."

Nobody who lived through the Depression will ever forget it.

In and around Monroe things were bad, but the majority of people still had some kind of job, and daily life was pretty much normal.

There was an inn in a neighboring county where many workmen ate breakfast and lunch, and which was run by a pleasant woman named Jane Kellogg. Her food was good, her prices were fair, and she was always a good "touch" for a small loan—if she knew you and you struck her as a decent person.

Jane's husband, Earle, was another matter. He was jealous of any man who smiled at his wife. He embarrassed Jane constantly by arguing with her customers, most of whom left him alone because Earle was not only angry but violent. Stories of his fistfights were legendary. He was the playground bully who never grew up.

Sometimes, it was later said, he heard voices telling him that his wife was being unfaithful. And sometimes when he spoke, when he accused her to her face of such betrayals, a voice came from him that was not his. He felt as if someone else had begun to speak through him . . . as if he were a marionette being manipulated by someone else.

One day, when he was putting on a necktie for a civic function he was to attend, he stared at his hand in the mirror. The hand knotting his tie was not . . . his own.

He saw liver spots and gnarled arthritic knuckles and heavy white hair.

He quickly raised his other hand and compared the two. One of the hands was not his.

And then he raised his eyes and stared at his face—but it was not his face.

For only a brief moment, he saw the face of another man—a very old, angry, and evil man—inside his own face.

He opened his mouth to speak, and a voice not his own at all uttered the words, "The harlot must be punished!"

It is said that Earle never discussed any of this until after the events that led to his downfall. That was because he was ashamed and feared people would think he was insane.

Yet, by not seeking help. . . .

• • •

Today the stories of what led to the killing contradict each other. Some insist that Earle became psychotic when a man brought Jane a bouquet of flowers. Others insist that Earle got upset about something else entirely—that Jane had nothing to do with it.

This much is known: there was a local carpenter for whom Earle had developed an ominous hatred.

One day Earle lured the carpenter to a wooded nook across the street from Union Cemetery, knocked the man unconscious, and then set him on fire.

Earle fled the scene, hiding for a time in his basement, where it is rumored that the demon within him took over entirely—laughing about the burning man, promising to kill Earle's wife next.

When the police arrested him, Earle allegedly kept whispering to himself—or to a second person that nobody else could see.

The townspeople were outraged. Everybody called for the death penalty. Fairfield County had never known a crime this terrible.

In custody, Earle was unnaturally quiet. He told the police very little about himself, his motives in this case, or why he'd chosen a site directly across the street from Union Cemetery to kill the man.

But during and after the trial there was great speculation about Earle's attraction to Union Cemetery, with some, including his own kin, insisting that long before the murder Earle had developed a peculiar attraction to the old cemetery—and often drove over there to park and look at the headstones and the rustic New England setting.

Even today they insist that while Earle had always been a fighter, he had never been a killer . . . not before his visits to Union Cemetery took their toll.

Not before he was heard to speak in voices not his own—and to speak to a person nobody else could see.

The White Lady

A HOBO was passing through Monroe one nigh
and decided to sleep on the hill above Union Cemetery
It was the right night for sleeping outside—the temper
ature in the seventies, the stars out full and bright, an
the sweet smell of newly mown grass floating on the air

Just after ten the hobo unrolled his sleeping bag an
went to sleep.

Around midnight, however, he woke up withou
knowing quite why. He guessed it was because he wa
not a heavy sleeper. Distant cars and trains frequentl
awakened him.

He sat up, rubbing sleep from his eyes.

Below him spread Union Cemetery, shadowy an
dignified in the moonlight.

Inevitably, sight of a graveyard caused the hobo
think of his own demise someday. He had a so

somewhere whom he wanted to say goodbye to before his own time came.

And then the hobo saw the glow.

At first, he was not certain of what he was seeing—merely an elongated glow that seemed to be flitting through the tombstones.

He stood up, fascinated, walking swiftly down the hill through the newly mown grass.

By now, he saw that the glow was actually a woman dressed in a veil and wedding gown—of a style from the last century.

Around the woman moved many small, dark shapes.

The hobo could hear the woman speaking . . . as if she were arguing with the shapes.

And then, as suddenly as she'd appeared, the White Lady vanished, taking the dark shapes with her.

The hobo never forgot his encounter with the White Lady . . . nor have the dozens of other people who've had similar encounters with her.

Given the nature of ghosts—people who have often suffered tragedies and who therefore remain rooted to the area where the tragedy took place—it is reasonable to assume that the White Lady was a resident of the area and that some terrible fate overtook her.

For the past several decades, the people in and around Monroe have seen the Lady.

Indeed, when Ed and Lorraine advertised in the newspaper that they wanted to speak to anybody who'd seen the Lady, many, many people phoned and wrote, eager to tell their stories.

Among the people who shared their stories with the Warrens were the Barberri brothers, Frank and Vincent.

Today, Frank is a retired Connecticut state trooper. Vincent lives in the South.

"We lived in a house above Union Cemetery," Frank notes. "And one spring night, when we were boys, we were down in the cemetery playing when we saw this very bright light. In the middle of the light was this very attractive woman.

"She was very close . . . no more than two hundred yards away. We stopped playing and just stared at her as she floated through the cemetery."

"She wasn't alone," Vincent says. "There were these dark forms around her and they seemed to be arguing with the woman. She was dressed in an old-fashioned veil and a full wedding gown."

Frightened, the boys ran up the hill and tried to get their parents to come down and see the Lady in the cemetery.

Their father just shrugged. He thought the boys had just gotten overexcited and were imagining things.

Their mother, always a good sport, went down to the cemetery, but when she got there, the Lady was gone.

When their mother saw headlights sweep over the cemetery, she said that that was what the boys had probably seen—headlights. And nothing more.

Night after night, the boys sat at their bedroom window, looking for the White Lady to appear again. Seeing her had been eerie, and yet it was an experience they wanted to have again.

Years later, when he was a young man, Vincent did see the Lady again. In fact, he saw her twice.

"One night I was sitting on a ledge up across from the cemetery—I sat there a lot of times so I could look for deer to shoot—and when I looked down into the cemetery . . . I saw the White Lady.

"This time there didn't seem to be anybody with

her—no dark form or anything—and no sound of arguing, either.

"She moved up the driveway toward the entrance to the cemetery—I could see her very clearly—and then vanished . . . just like smoke."

On another occasion, Vincent was coming home late one night, and there, just off the road, he saw the Lady in the cemetery again. No voices this time, either. Just the shimmering white light with the Lady in the middle of it.

There are many tales of the White Lady, perhaps the oddest being of the man who went to the cemetery late one night to speak with his recently buried wife. Just by kneeling at his wife's grave, the man felt as if she were with him again.

This particular night, however, as he knelt there in the chill autumn night, dead leaves scraping across the gravestones surrounding him, a great sorrow filled him . . . and as he looked up from his wife's grave, he saw the White Lady standing there, watching him.

"I wish my husband would have loved me as much as you love your wife," she said.

And then she was gone, leaving him alone in the midnight graveyard, and to his own grief and loss.

Strange Passenger

IMAGINE THIS. It is late at night. You're driving on a dark, deserted highway.

Even though it is a warm summer night and the moon is bright, something is making you nervous.

Maybe it's the fact that you haven't seen another car in the past ten minutes. Maybe it's the fact that there's a curious chill in the car. And a sour, gassy smell.

You want to be home. With your wife and children. Sitting in your living room. Laughing along with Jay Leno.

You speed up a little. Sure you're doing ten miles per hour over the posted speed limit, but who's going to notice?

Anyway, getting a speeding ticket might not be so bad. At least you'd see another human being.

"I used to get scared when I drove this road at night, too."

Your head snaps rightward. You're traveling alone. Who could possibly have spoken?

And then you see him. Man in a shabby suit. Eerie gray eyes.

"Someday you'll be like I am now," the shabby man says in a chilling voice. "And then nothing will scare you."

Instinctively, you slam on the brakes. Turn off the engine. Open the door and jump out, leaving your car in the middle of the road.

Behind the glowing headlights, you can still see him. The man who suddenly appeared in your car. He is leaning out the window, shouting for you to come back.

You start running, out of breath already, and you begin staggering down the center of the road when a car appears. Coming fast. Rock music blaring out the open windows.

You run toward it. Waving your arms for help.

Car slams on his brakes.

"Hey, Pops, what happened, your date get away from you?" the driver said.

The other three boys in the car, just as drunk as the driver, start to laugh.

They're not going to be any help at all.

You wave them on.

They pull past you, laying down rubber, the rock music fading into the night.

You don't know what to do now except stand there in the middle of this wooded highway.

Who was the man in your car? How did he get there?

And then you see it. And can't believe it.

Your own car.

Coming slowly toward you.

With the ghoul behind the wheel.

He pulls up alongside you.

Smiles with rotted black teeth. "You may not believe this, but someday you'll be just like me."

And then—

He's gone.

Gone.

And you're left standing there on this deserted midnight road, looking at your own car, engine throbbing, headlights stabbing into the gloom.

You get in. Drive home.

And never forget what happened.

This is just one of the many incidents reported about the road running past Union Cemetery. The man to whom it happened has asked that his name not be used.

But another man is quite willing to step forward and talk about his phantom encounter.

Rod Vecsey works for a lumber supply company, a job some find curious because Rod won the Connecticut state lottery, which was then worth $2.5 million dollars. He works, he says, to keep busy. Rod has a handsome home, a wife and two children, and spends much of his free time using his artistic talents, which are considerable.

Here, in Rod's own words, is his story.

I've always liked the night shift at the lumber company. For one thing, the pay is a little better and the people are a little nicer.

There's just something about the evening shift that seems to bring all the workers a little closer together, sort of like a family.

This was summer 1991.

After work, which was usually right about midnight, I'd stand in the parking lot smoking a cigarette with the guys. Then we'd say good night, toss our empty lunch buckets into our cars, and ride off.

On this particular night there'd been a hot, steamy summer rain earlier so the humidity was pretty bad. And there was a lot of knee-high ground fog scudding across the lot. It had a thick, unreal texture, I remember, like something you see in a movie.

I took a different route home that night, one that would give me some extra driving time in the new Chevrolet.

Actually, once you got over the humidity, it was a beautiful night, late June with a full moon and the forest of ash and beech and birch trees beautiful in the silver light.

The disk jockey was doing some kind of tribute to Bruce Springsteen, a singer I happen to like a lot, so I nudged up the volume on the radio and enjoyed myself as I moved along Route 59, going past Union Cemetery on my left.

The only thing that bothered me was the ground fog. I finally snapped on the yellow fog lights.

And then suddenly I had this terrible feeling of not being alone any more.

You know how you sometimes get suspicious that maybe somebody's crouched down and hiding in your backseat?

Slowing the car, I looked over at what I assumed would be an empty seat. But there was a man sitting there. But there was no way a man could have climbed into my car while the car was moving!

He might have been a hobo of some kind because his

floppy brown hat and wrinkled brown suit and the stubble on his face suggested somebody who hadn't had any luck in a long time. He turned his head and stared at me.

I was almost mesmerized by his presence but then I had to look back at the road.

I turned off the radio, wanting total concentration.

The road that runs past Union Cemetery is almost like a country lane. The trees on either side give it an air of a lane through a park. Not even the swirling fog, as eerie as it was that night, could detract from the Connecticut beauty of the scene.

Or so I thought, anyway.

A hundred feet away, standing in the direct center of the road, stood a woman dressed in a shabby old nightgown that was little more than tatters in places. Her dark hair tumbled well past her shoulders. Her eyes glowed with a curious blue radiance that brought back my goosebumps.

She raised a slender arm and put up a hand, palm forward, demanding that I stop.

I slammed on the brakes, feeling the rear end start to fishtail on the fog-slicked black top. I glanced rightward—the man was gone!

Then I yelled through the open window for the woman to get out of the way, but if she heard me she didn't let on.

I passed right through her. That's the only way to describe it. I didn't have time to stop. My car pushed right on through her body, and I could feel the icy cold of her touching my right shoulder and cheek.

I managed to slam the car to a stop.

At first, all I could do was sit there and shake. My entire right leg, all the way up to the hip, trembled with a force I couldn't control, not even when I clamped both hands on it.

I looked at her in the rearview mirror, through wisps of fog.

I saw now that the bodice of her nightgown was of a very old-fashioned style, one worn well over a hundred years ago. A brooch, also of that era, hung from a golden chain around her neck.

All I could think was that I was having a breakdown of some kind—first a man abruptly appearing inside my car, and then a woman who hadn't even blinked when my car passed right through her!

There was a peculiar odor at that time, too, not so much of something rotten but rather of something dusty, something that had been closed up a long time, like a piece of clothing kept in a small attic for decades.

And then she turned and walked to the front of the car again.

Moments later, she was retreating down the road, a lonely figure lost in the fog and gloom of night.

I shouted at her to stop, told her I wanted to help her.

But then she was gone.

The last glimpse I had of her, she was walking down the hill toward the Episcopal Church . . . her night-gown hanging in tatters from her seared flesh.

Sometime during all this, my car had died. I now reached down to the ignition, about to turn the engine over again, when the sorrow came.

That's the right word for it. Sorrow. Grief beyond imagining. A melancholy so deep that it literally para-lyzed me.

I sat there, totally unable even to turn the key in the ignition.

All I could do was give myself over to the terrible sorrow I wanted so desperately to escape.

I don't know how long I sat there. I do know that a car came along and abruptly pulled out around me, its horn blaring angrily.

I gathered myself as best I could and drove home.

Ordinarily, my wife waits up for me, with a sandwich and a beer on the kitchen table.

But tonight I was beyond the pleasures of food and drink.

Without a word, I went into our bedroom and lay on the bed and began sobbing like a small child whose parent has just died.

My wife did all she could, held me and kissed me and listened patiently to my story of what had happened tonight.

But not until two weeks later, when a friend suggested that we talk with Ed and Lorraine Warren, not until then did we understand exactly what had taken place on that lonely stretch of road by Union Cemetery.

I had come in contact with a dead person and it had been too much for me to deal with, which was what my sadness had been all about. I was sharing the sorrow that the dead woman had for some reason taken into eternity with her.

My life has not been the same since. Despite some very good fortune, I have never been able to forget that night, or the feelings it evoked in me.

As Lorraine Warren said to me recently, "Sometimes a paranormal experience gives us an insight into ourselves that we almost can't handle."

I think this is most definitely true in my case.

Videotaping a Ghost

WHY DO ghosts glow? Lorraine and I are often asked that question. We believe that ghosts draw electromagnetic energy from the plant life, trees, and bushes and that this energy is one of the reasons they often project a brilliant light. Indoors, ghosts draw on human sources for their energy and their glow.

We're also asked about "ghost lights" that resemble tiny white balloons. Many people report seeing these in photographs they've taken at graveyards. The curious thing is, the "lights" can be seen only on film, not by the naked eye. We've seen dozens of such photographs. We feel they're a supernatural phenomenon associated with graveyards where spirit activity is constant.

I mention these things because they demonstrate that the processes used by the Society are scientific whenever possible.

Before starting a serious investigation into Union

Cemetery, for instance, one of our researchers spent a great number of hours there with his tape recorder. This man, who is quite well educated and who was at first skeptical of occult matters, has developed a system all his own to get "soundings" in graveyards.

He went to Union several days running. He would kneel by a gravestone and say a prayer and then speak the name on the gravestone. He said that he wanted to pray for the dead person and relay any messages to the person's living relatives.

One day, his tape recorder running, he was able to capture the sound of the spirit saying "23" again and again—the number of years she'd been dead.

This man's early work on behalf of the Society helped convince us that Union would be a place worth studying.

Indeed, soon after the man had his experience with "23" repeated over and over, I started bringing my video recorder to the cemetery.

And on the night of September 1, at 2:40 A.M., my patience paid off.

For six nights previous I'd come out to the graveyard and parked. Each night I followed the same procedure. I brought along all my video gear, and when I got there, I set up a tripod in the cemetery, keeping the camera inside with me. With the tripod ready to use, I could mount the camera and be taping in moments.

September 1 began like all the other nights. I heard the kind of whispers common to graveyards—there are many more unsettled souls than most people realize— and I saw flashes of ghost lights. I had already video-taped the latter and audiotaped the former. Tonight wanted more, much more.

But by 2:30 I have to admit, I was getting discouraged. Some projects just never work out. Maybe this would be one of them. Maybe my instincts were wrong. Maybe I was never going to get any dramatic evidence from Union Cemetery.

All that changed abruptly when the ghost lights, which are strange luminescent glows, grew brighter. Suddenly everything was unnaturally silent except for the incessant crickets.

I knew something was about to happen.

I grabbed my camera, jumped out of the van, and ran to the tripod. In moments I was recording the glow directly in front of me, the glow that eventually took the shape of a woman.

I put her age at thirty. She had dark hair and wore a flowing white gown.

The White Lady wasn't alone. There were dark figures surrounding her, shapes that seemed to jump on her. I realized that as long ago as fifty years people had reported seeing this woman and the wood ghosts who engulfed her and who seemed to be arguing with her.

And I was capturing it on videotape!

She was walking directly toward me, this ghostly figure whose light glowed bright in the dark graveyard, the fabled White Lady.

She was walking directly toward me, yes, but when I tried to see her in the camera's viewfinder, she wasn't there!

The sounds of the wood ghosts grew angrier and more oppressive. Whatever argument they were having with the woman was certainly continuing.

Now I stepped out from the camera and started walking toward her.

I was frightened and unsure of what to do but I kept walking straight ahead.

And then she was gone!

The woman was gone and the wood ghosts were gone and their noises were gone.

I was standing in the center of a darkened graveyard once more, my entire body covered with frozen sweat, the crickets almost comically loud in my ears.

Then I remembered the camera.

If I hadn't been able to see the woman in the view-finder, would I have her on tape?

I quickly packed up the car and drove straight home.

When the tape was ready to view, I remember thinking that this was going to be my biggest accomplishment or my greatest folly.

What would the tape hold for me?

Several members of the Society joined me in that first viewing, and as the tape began to roll and images appeared on the screen, a whoop of excitement came up from the people around me.

Because there, right there on tape for everybody to see, was the Lady!

The videotape footage turned out incredibly well and offers incontrovertible proof to any doubters that the spirit world is in constant contact with our own world.

But as fulfilling as my encounter with the Lady had been, Union Cemetery held another great adventure for me. . . .

A Visit with the Dead

THE STORY goes this way: a man got up in the middle of the night to get a glass of water. As he passed through the darkened house, he thought he saw something odd in the dining room—a lovely young woman sitting at the end of the dining table, watching him. "Hello, David," she said. At first, he did not recognize her. Her features were oddly distorted, like something seen through an out-of-focus lens. He walked toward her. She held out her hand to him. Her hand went right through him. He began to sweat and shake, feeling as if he were trapped in a nightmare. "It's just me, David, your first wife, Claire." And so it was—Claire—dead now for seventeen years from a tragic fire. She had come back to see him.

I had an experience like this myself, one time in Union Cemetery when I was out looking for "gravestone images," those patterns of lichen and age that sometimes appear to be faces of people, the way ink-blots do. But they shift quickly, changing all the time. That's what makes the whole "gravestone images" business amazing. You have to be there at exactly the right time.

Anyway, that's what I was doing in Union Cemetery that sunny autumn afternoon. The graveyard was empty.

I was bending down and adjusting my camera to take the first tombstone shot when all of a sudden I heard behind me a woman's voice say, "Taking pictures of ghosts?"

I stood up and turned around and here was this well-dressed woman . . . so well-dressed that she even wore high-heels in the middle of this cemetery. There was no car around . . . nobody with her . . . and I thought, what is this woman doing out in a rural graveyard all by herself like this?

I'd been riding my motorcycle that day, and I had on a sweatshirt and a pair of jeans and boots. Pretty scruffy-looking, in other words. And I thought, this woman sure takes chances—she has no idea who I am; I could be a rapist or something—but she speaks to me anyway.

But I kept hearing the echoes of her voice in my ears. It was very familiar . . . and so, in a certain way, was her face. But she had these wide dark sunglasses on, and they sort of hid her face.

And then I realized that this woman looked like Ethyl Whittaker . . . a woman who had died four years before . . . a woman who came to our Psychic Society years earlier and introduced herself as a psychic photographer after a lecture we'd given at a local club.

She came up and showed us a photo she'd taken one

day of her husband working in the driveway. Their dog was with him. It was a new home. There were no other homes on the street, and nobody in the photo except her husband. Yet when Ethyl had the film developed, there was a transparent image of a little girl and boy. Now the camera couldn't have double-exposed. Impossible. But the images of the little girl and boy were very clear. The girl wore a white blouse and a black jacket and a short skirt coming down to her knees. Her brother was sitting on a tricycle right alongside her. If you just glanced at the photo without really examining it, you'd say this was a double exposure. But it wasn't. In fact, what we found out was that these two children had died in a drowning accident over thirty years earlier. We found this out through investigation and psychometry, which is the ability of somebody to hold a photo or item belonging to somebody else—and to instantly know many things about that other person.

This is how we learned that Ethyl was a psychic photographer.

Ethyl had gone into many homes with us after this and taken photos of ghosts and apparitions. And then unfortunately, when she reached seventy, she developed cancer and died.

A few nights before she died, she'd been in a coma. Lorraine visited her a few times but Ethyl was generally incoherent, so much so that Lorraine walked in one night and started to straighten the covers and Ethyl said, "Oh, you don't need to do that. Lorraine will take care of all my needs." Lorraine and Ethyl were very good friends. And of course Lorraine tried to comfort the husband, too. He was just devastated by his wife's illness.

Everybody who knew Ethyl was having a hard time

dealing with Ethyl's dying because she'd always been such a good person. She never forgot your birthday, for instance, always baking you a cake and putting your name on it.

One night around 7:30 the phone rang. Now remember, Ethyl had been in a comatose state for two weeks . . . but here she was on the other end of the line as rational and cheery as she'd been as a healthy young woman. "Hi, Ed, how are you?" And I said, "Who is this?" And she said, "It's Ethyl." "Ethyl Whittaker?"

Lorraine: "I picked up the other phone when I heard Ed say this because I was shocked. I'd seen Ethyl only a day ago and she was deep in a coma. Very deep. This couldn't possibly be her on the phone—and yet it was. She said, 'I must have been sleeping for the last couple of weeks and now I'm just waking up.'"

When we hung up, we immediately called Ethyl's husband and told him what had happened. He said it was impossible. Ethyl was near death. He called the hospital. They told him that Ethyl was still in a coma and had been all day and night.

Of course, we knew of similar experiences where dying people who were supposedly incapable of even opening their eyes had phoned loved ones to say goodbye.

Anyway, this was the background going through my mind when I stood in the cemetery that afternoon and stared at the strange, well-dressed woman. "Are you interested in taking pictures of tombstones and graveyards?" And she laughed.

"I know I don't look like it but I'm the director of the New England Society for Psychic Research."

She laughed softly. "But, Ed, you always look like this."

She then said she was interested in epitaphs and the histories of graveyards.

And as she spoke, I thought, My God, this is Ethyl Whittaker. But I couldn't say that, of course. "Are you Ethyl Whittaker, who died four years ago?" You just don't blurt out things like that.

Then she glanced at her watch and said, "Oh, dear, I've got to get home and make my husband's dinner." And Ethyl would always say things like that because Ethyl was always late getting around to things. She was one of those people who moved by her own internal clock.

She started to turn around and walk away and I said, "Would you mind if I take a picture of you?"

She said, "No, I don't mind."

She was heading over to a group of trees that was about thirty yards away. "Is that where your car is?" I said. I couldn't believe it. There was a road over there, but before you got to the road you had to go through trees and a swamp and a barbed wire fence.

She turned fully around for me to take her picture.

"Would you mind taking off your sunglasses?" I said.

She took them off.

And then, when I saw her eyes, I knew it was Ethyl Whittaker. A person can change in many ways but the eyes never change. And that was the case here, and now I was certain it was Ethyl.

Then Ethyl started walking toward these trees—the same trees where earlier a picture of an apparition, the White Lady of Union Cemetery, was also taken—so I jumped on my bike because I wanted to get over to the road where she said her car was parked.

It only took me forty or fifty seconds to get around there.

But there was no car there—and suddenly Ethyl was gone. Vanished.

Was it really Ethyl?

I genuinely believe it was.

Yes. She appeared in daylight in full physical form. This was the first time I'd ever experienced anything like that . . . especially with a dear friend like Ethyl.

Ed and Lorraine Warren

Over the past three years our Society has collected more than two dozen verified stories of tragedies that have taken place in and around Union Cemetery.

There were the two young girls killed in a car accident right in front of the cemetery; the man who committed suicide by using dynamite; the terrible demonic possession of an 11-year-old boy; the woman who tried to stab her husband in the middle of the night for no apparent reason—all reflect the curious influence of the cemetery . . . what psychic investigators recognize as an "aura of disaster."

Certainly, this cemetery has that aura, particularly when you look into its background.

The New England Society for Psychic Research will continue to investigate every letter and phone call it receives relevant to the cemetery.

We only hope that the violent events of the past will no longer exact the same human toll on the people who live in the area.

INCIDENTS
AT OTHER
GRAVEYARDS

Other stories submitted to the New England
Society for Psychic Research, being addi-
tional proof of life beyond the grave as experienced by both the living and the dead.

In horror movies the spookiest scenes frequently take place in graveyards.

There are good reasons why. Spirits often roam graveyards. By this we don't mean terrible monsters—though occasionally you see such a monster in a graveyard—we simply mean the spirits of dead people who wish to make contact again with living people.

Our Society receives many phone calls and letters from people eager to share their experiences with us. We've selected several of those experiences and turned them into the second part of this book.

At a recent lecture we were asked how it is that so many graveyards seem to be haunted.

Our reply: "On a lark, people frequently go to nearby graveyards and begin performing all sorts of dark rites that they've read about in books. These people think they're just *having a little fun. But what they're really doing is inviting satanic forces into the graveyard . . . and into their lives."*

For this reason, we urge you not to experiment with any occult rites a friend or a book may have led you to.

You have only to look at the shocking number of satanic murders in the United States to see how serious a problem this has become . . . and several of those murders have taken place in cemeteries.

Here, then, are some further experiences set in the graveyards of New England.

—Ed and Lorraine Warren

The Man Who
Knew Everything

IN AN otherwise unremarkable New England town at the end of the last decade, there was a local talkshow host, named David Ahearne, who was happy to inform most of his callers that they didn't know what they were talking about.

David Ahearne knew everything—they knew nothing—and they should consider it an honor that he let them talk to him at all. This was the impression he gave, anyway.

The owner of the station loved the show. In the two years Ahearne had been on the air here, the ratings for this time slot had quadrupled, and new advertisers were constantly being added.

But not everybody shared the owner's enthusiasm for Ahearne.

If you were a shy or timid caller, he took you apart in the most humiliating way.

If you disagreed with him politically, he usually implied that you were a pervert or a foreign agent of some kind.

Many of his listeners loved to hear the other callers debased. They were the sort of listeners who spent a lot of time in front of their TVs watching professional wrestling.

There were a lot of people Ahearne seemed to hate, but there were none he hated more than those callers who expressed a belief in the supernatural.

"I'll tell you what," he'd said to such a caller, "you bring a ghostie or a goblin to my radio studio, and I'll put him on the air." Then he'd cackle. "No, I'll even do better than that! I'll turn my show over to him for an entire day!"

His true-blue fans loved this kind of sarcasm. This is why they listened. Hearing sad or despondent or slightly crazed people made them feel much better about themselves and their own dreary lot.

On one of those spring afternoons when you want to be outdoors, Ahearne was in his familiar radio studio spewing out his familiar venom.

The calls had been running to the standard themes— one man insisted he'd been taken to Venus in a space-ship; another man insisted that in a previous life, he'd been Spartacus; and a woman was telling everybody that the radon inspectors people let into their basements were actually government agents affixing listening de-vices to the walls.

Ahearne was having a great time with all of them.

Then the little girl called.

Ahearne was not used to hearing a child's voice on his incoming speaker.

The girl sounded no older than six or seven. She spoke so softly that he could scarcely hear her.

"We're waiting for you, Mr. Ahearne."

Ahearne knew he needed to be careful. It would be unseemly of him to bully a child.

"Who's waiting for me, dear?"

"Us."

"And who is 'us' exactly, darlin'?"

"The people in the graveyard."

Ahearne laughed. Couldn't help himself. "You live in a graveyard?"

"Yes. With my friends."

"This is better than going to Venus on a starship!" Ahearne said.

"She isn't making a joke." This voice belonged to an old man. "We really do live in the graveyard."

"Sounds like a pretty lively group to me!" Ahearne laughed. "But remember, gags like this get real old real fast—so why don't you just hang up now, all right, folks?"

"We want you to come visit us," said a third voice, a woman's. "We want to show you that you shouldn't make fun of supernatural things."

"Boy, oh, boy, are these people going to get obnoxious!" Ahearne said. "Why don't we break for a commercial and when we get back—they'll be gone! I promise you!"

When the commercial started rolling, and Ahearne could no longer be heard on the air, he said into the phone, "Whoever the hell you are, you've worn out your welcome. Now hang up the phone and let somebody else use this line."

This time the little girl spoke. "We didn't want to call but he asked us to."

"And now I'm supposed to say 'Who is he?' Right?"

"Your son. Robert. He'll be in Hillpointe Cemetery tonight, waiting for you."

Then she broke the connection.

Ahearne sat there staring at the phone. Nobody in this town knew about Robert. Nobody.

Hillpointe Cemetery was on the edge of town. Mostly poor people and immigrants were buried here, people whose family dated back to the second wave of settlers, the ragtag group that had come after the Puritans.

Ahearne almost never visited this section of the town. He'd grown up poor, in a shabby household made violent by his father's constant drinking, and now that he was successful—successful enough, at any rate, to drive a new Continental and live in a posh condo—he did not want to be reminded of his depressing origins.

At forty-two years of age, Ahearne had been many places, including a brief radio stint in Miami during which he'd fallen in love with a beautiful society woman who'd constantly assured him that she was in the process of getting a divorce from her powerful husband.

One summer night she confided to him that she was pregnant and that the child was his but that she would tell her husband that he was the father.

Ahearne was crushed by this. He'd always wanted a child. But not under these circumstances.

The woman never did leave her husband. Indeed, during the middle of her pregnancy, they reconciled. He bought her an even bigger house in an even more prestigious neighborhood.

She ceased seeing Ahearne entirely. Said it was better this way.

But what about the baby? he'd said.

He'll never know about you, she said. If he did, he'd just be confused and bitter.

He never saw or spoke to the woman again.

But somehow, six years later, she tracked him down and sent him a brief, curt note:

Dear David,

I'm sorry I have to tell you this but I felt you deserved to know—Robert was drowned yesterday in a boating accident.

Sincerely,
Jane

Following this, Ahearne worked his way through a number of radio stations and an even greater number of women. He told nobody of Robert. He never had.

Yet now, all these years later, somebody had found out about Robert and was using his memory to hurt Ahearne.

But who could it be?

Who could possibly know?

And, what did they want? Blackmail?

That evening, before going to the cemetery, Ahearne had had a dinner date with a very nice but slightly dull woman he'd been seeing. She was one of those women he wanted to fall in love with—she was, in his mother's words, "sensible"—but there were no sparks.

He took her to the town's nicest restaurant, where several people came over and asked for his autograph, and several more stopped by to slap him on the back and tell him how much fun his show was.

All these years Ahearne had waited for recognition like this . . . and for a radio station where management was afraid of him . . . but now that he had it, he found it empty.

He kept thinking of the call this afternoon.

What had the little girl said? "Your son, Robert. He'll be in Hillpointe Cemetery tonight, waiting."

"Are you all right, David?" his dinner companion said, bringing him back to reality.

He smiled sadly. "Overworked and underpaid." He stubbed out his cigarette. "Would you mind if I took you home a little early tonight?"

She patted his hand. She was always understanding. To a fault. "That's fine. You look like you could use some sleep."

"Thanks."

He helped her on with her wrap and then took her home.

So now here he was. Hillpointe Cemetery.

A brambly hill covered with modest white gravestones blanched white by the moonlight. Just over the hill, at the roundhouse, he could hear freight cars banging together. The odor from the nearby sewage treatment plant made him sick briefly. Even in death the residents of Hillpointe had to put up with intolerable conditions.

He wasn't sure what he was looking for. He felt foolish even being here.

Robert was dead, killed in a boating accident. . . .

He stood there, smoking three cigarettes quickly, for the next fifteen minutes.

He saw nothing except the weed-cluttered graveyard and the graffiti-covered tombstones.

And then, down the hill near the iron gates, standing perfectly still in the pale moonlight—

He saw a young boy dressed in a red-and-white striped T-shirt and jeans and tennis shoes.

The boy was ash-blond, like his mother, and yet as David Ahearne stared at him, he was able to see his own face in the boy's. . . .

Ahearne started down the hill. "Robert?"

The boy continued to stare at him.

"Are you Robert?"

The boy nodded.

Now that he was drawing near, Ahearne saw that he could see through the boy—that Robert looked to be an apparition and not a real boy at all, like an image projected on a screen.

Ahearne stopped, suddenly afraid.

He glanced around the cemetery. He wanted reassurance that he was not caught up in some kind of nightmare.

He felt his entire body begin to stiffen in fear. Suddenly the graveyard seemed to fall away and he seemed to be standing on a plane that was not of earth—

No sound of freight cars coupling. No smells from the sewage treatment plant.

Where was he?

Where was the real world?

The boy grew larger—seemed to move closer—and yet he had not really moved at all.

"You're my father."

Ahearne nodded. "Yes, I guess I am."

"And you're afraid."

"Yes. Yes, yes, I am."

"But it's not me or the netherworld you're afraid of."

"It's not?"

"No. You're afraid of yourself. Of your own loneliness—that's why you make fun of the people who call in. They have lives and you don't."

The boy put forth his hand. At first, Ahearne was afraid to reach out and touch it but he did.

His fingers felt as if he'd dipped them in warm honey—a feeling of peace and well-being spread through his entire body.

He enjoyed the sensation so much that he closed his eyes and let himself be overcome with love for the son he'd never seen before.

"I love you, Robert," he said.

"I love you, too, Father. And I want you to be happy."

Ahearne remained this way for several minutes. He had never before experienced the nurturing care of having someone love him the way his son loved him. For the first time in his life he felt as if his existence had purpose, meaning, dignity.

And then the sensation of well-being was gone.

The earthly night returned piece by piece—

—first the train cars clanking

—then the smell of the sewage plant

—then the thorny tangle of weeds clinging to his legs by the path leading to the iron gates.

He was alone again—alone in a vast universe that frightened and depressed him.

But then he thought of Robert. He had actually seen the boy. He was sure of it.

And Robert had actually given him some clues about living . . . about how his life needed to be changed.

Standing there in the moonlit cemetery, Ahearne knew that his life would never be the same again.

He was a changed man.

Ed Warren

There's long been a debate about apparitions. The mainstream scientific community argues that they are little more than projections of a person's own mind. If you have been thinking of your cousin, say—consciously or unconsciously—your cousin might well appear to you as an apparition.

The Ahearne case was more complex because it also involved spirits contacting Ahearne in his radio studio.

But I've always been taken with Nandor Fodor's comment in *An Encyclopedia of Psychic Science:*

"The driving motive [behind an apparition] is usually an urgent message of extreme danger, illness or death on the part of the agent. But it is also often a warning of impending danger of death of someone closely related to the percipient."

When we received Mr. Ahearne's letter asking us to help explain his meeting with Robert, I immediately thought of the Fodor quote and its application to Mr. Ahearne.

There are two kinds of death—physical and spiritual.

Mr. Ahearne was in the process of losing his soul . . . of dying spiritually. And so his son, the son he'd never known before, interceded to show Mr. Ahearne the right and true way to live life.

Today, Mr. Ahearne lives in Scottsdale, Arizona, is married and the father of two boys, and works as a newspaper advertising salesman. He owes his newfound happiness to a young man named Robert . . . a young man who returned to earth to perform an act of kindness.

Sexual Demons

SEVENTEEN-YEAR-old Jamie O'Malley should have been a popular senior at St. Joseph's High School. He was good-looking, intelligent, and the only son of a prosperous local banker and his socially active wife.

But unknown to his classmates, Jamie O'Malley had spent two of the past four summers in mental hospitals where he'd been treated for depression both with drugs and with electroshock therapy. During the school year he retreated to the comfort and privacy of his parents' Victorian mansion near New York City.

For five years Jamie had been frequently taken to New York, where he underwent analysis with prominent psychiatrists. None found any psychological reasons for his depression. It was assumed, therefore, that Jamie's problems were chemical. At the time, 1979, genetic causes of depression were just being recognized by the mainstream medical community.

Jamie was treated with experimental drugs. After a few months he became a much happier young man.

Ten years earlier, Jamie O'Malley had been left in the care of a nanny named Felice DuBois. Only later did Jamie's parents learn that all of Ms. DuBois's nanny "credentials" were forged.

For their twentieth wedding anniversary, David O'Malley decided to take his wife on a month-long European vacation and leave Jamie in the care of his new nanny, Felice. If the nanny had any problems or questions, she could simply turn to the rest of the three-person staff—a maid, a butler, and a hired man. They could help her. And David planned to phone three or four times a week. Everything would be fine.

At this point in his young life, Jamie O'Malley was a very active and outgoing boy. He spent sunny summer days playing baseball, riding his bike through the beautiful Connecticut hills, and inviting less fortunate friends of his over to play in the swimming pool.

At least, this is what he did when his parents were around. Felice DuBois had other ideas. She frequently made him accompany her on shopping trips into town. She also dragged him along to afternoon movies at a nearby shopping mall—movies she wanted to see. And at night, after dinner, after the rest of the staff had retired, she made him go to bed early where she read to him from a most peculiar book—one that was all about demons and devils and the dark force called Lucifer.

But this wasn't all Felice did.

As she read, she took his young hand and touched it to her breast. Or dropped it lower so that Jamie's fingers felt the warmth of her inner thighs. Or took his fingers and touched them softly to her cheek. She was a very pretty young girl, very dark and shapely, and at first Jamie had had a youngster's crush on her.

But less than a week after his parents left, Jamie found himself afraid of the intense young woman. . . .

Late one rainy night he heard his bedroom door squeak open. He started to sit up in bed but he saw Felice in the doorway.

She was naked and carrying a candle in one hand and a painting of Lucifer performing vile sexual acts with several people.

Thinking Jamie asleep, Felice came to the edge of his bed and held the candle over his head and said, in a prayerful way, "Oh powerful Satan, I consecrate this young boy's life to your will."

Jamie kept his eyes closed tight for two reasons. One, he wasn't sure he should be looking at a naked woman. And two, he knew he would be in danger if she saw that he was awake.

The room suddenly grew colder. And a foul, fetid stench filled the room as Felice stood over him speaking in a tongue he did not understand.

"Take this boy, Satan! Make him your son!"

By now, Jamie was terrified of Felice and her peculiar behavior. He lay there, unmoving.

And then she was gone.

The room was dark again.

Moonlight filled the window; a soft, warm breeze fluttered the sheer curtain. It was as if Felice had never been there.

Four nights later, on the way back from a movie, Felice took a different way home.

"Did I ever tell you that I grew up near here?"

"No," Jamie said.

"Well, I did. And do you know where my favorite place was to play?"

"No."

"Over there."

Jamie turned and looked and was shocked. Felice had pointed to the graveyard, all silver and shadow in the moonlight.

"You played in a graveyard?"

"Yes."

"Why?"

"Because I—" She paused, obviously choosing her words carefully. "Are you tired?"

"Not real tired."

"Good. Let's pull over here."

She parked the car and they got out and drifted up the sloping grassy incline to the cemetery.

"Are you afraid?"

"Sort of," Jamie said.

"Take my hand then."

He took her hand and they walked the rest of the way to the cemetery.

When they reached a certain headstone, a massive piece of carven stone that reached back two centuries, she said, "Do you want to know a secret, Jamie?"

"I guess so." Actually, he wasn't sure. He was still very afraid of her.

"Touch the headstone."

"I'm afraid."

"There's nothing to be afraid of, Jamie."

"But I don't want to."

He couldn't see her face very well in the darkness, but he sensed her irritation with him.

"Do as I say, Jamie."

But she didn't wait any longer. She jerked his hand forward and touched his fingers to the headstone.

"Ow!" Jamie cried. The headstone was hot to the touch.

"You feel them, don't you?"

"Feel who?"

"The dead people in the earth. At night, when they're restless and roam the land, the headstones sometimes get hot."

"You're making that up."

"No, I'm not. That's how I first found out about— things, Jamie. One night when I was about your age, I snuck away from the house and came over here to play. And my dad came looking for me and I hid behind one of the headstones. And when I touched it—it was hot. Later that night, I came back."

"And you were only seven?"

"Yes. I had to sneak out but I came back because I knew I'd learn something."

"Learn what?"

"How to speak with the dead."

Jamie said nothing.

"You think I'm making that up, don't you?"

"Uh-huh."

"How would you like to speak with the dead?"

"I want to go home, Felice. I'm tired now."

"No, you're not. You're just afraid. I was afraid, too, Jamie, until I knew the truth. Now put your hand back up there on that headstone."

"No!"

She slapped him so hard he was momentarily blinded. He felt his cheeks burn and his eyes run with tears.

She took his hand and guided it to the headstone.

The young boy would never forget what he felt—the

entire ground shaking, as if an earthquake had been localized right there around the headstone. Also, from deep within the bowels of the earth, he heard the rumble of voices calling out his name—"Jamie! Jamie! Jamie!"

"They want to be your friends," Felice shouted above the sounds of the voices and the trembling of the earth.

Jamie was never to remember anything else about that night . . . nothing specific, anyway. Later on, he did recall fainting and crumbling to the ground. He also remembered the sensation of freezing and then of the voices in the ground growing deeper and stranger and more frightening.

A few hours later, he stirred, opened his eyes, and found himself in his own bedroom, in his own bed.

Silhouetted against the moonlit window was Felice. She was naked once more—and holding a butcher knife.

On the floor was a metal casting of Lucifer's horned head. Inside the casting a small candle glowed.

Felice slashed the knife across her forearm. She groaned—but it was a groan of pleasure, not pain—and then took her forearm and rubbed the open wound across her naked breasts, feeding the breasts with her own blood.

She then leaned over and let several drops of blood fall from her arm into the flame itself.

For a moment the candle went dark—but then it burst into an eerie green flame that painted the entire room an ugly lime color.

Jamie wondered if he was dreaming, but then he saw Felice slowly begin to dance around the candle as if in response to some primitive music only she could hear. . . .

Young as he was, Jamie knew that the gyrations of Felice's body suggested something sinful.

In the middle of her dance she raised the knife to slash her other arm. She again rubbed the wound against her breasts and continued to dance, throwing her head back as if in a kind of insane ecstasy. . . .

He was never sure when she went. All he knew was that dawn brought chill rain and complete exhaustion.

When he was in the bathroom brushing his teeth, the maid knocked and said, "Jamie, have you seen Felice this morning?"

"No, ma'am."

"Thank you."

The rest of the day, the maid and the butler searched the house and grounds for any sign of Felice—but she was gone.

Her nicely appointed efficiency apartment above the garage had been cleaned out thoroughly. Nothing of hers remained. It was as if she'd never been there at all.

The maid notified the police and an investigation began. Two weeks later, just as Jamie's parents returned home, the local chief of police concluded that no foul play had been involved—Felice DuBois had, for whatever reason, tired of her job and left the area.

Lorraine Warren

Several years ago we published a book called *The Haunted*, which was the true story of a Pennsylvania family that had found their house infested with demons.

During this time, we were reading Hal N. Banks' fine book, *An Introduction to Psychic Studies*, and came upon the following quote from an M.D. named E. N. Webster:

"At times I even hear [spirits'] voices. Insane people who are spoken of as hopelessly insane are frequently lost under the overwhelming control of a spirit or crowd of spirits. We frequently find by post-mortem examination that no physical disorder exists in the brain or nervous system of such persons."

I remembered this quote again when I was told Jamie's story.

Felice was obviously possessed by demons. As Dr. Webster noted, people such as Jamie are not insane but simply "under the overwhelming control of a spirit."

If Felice is alive today, and has not sought the help of a priest or minister, then she is likely seducing other young boys . . . and offering their bodies and souls to Satan.

The Unseen Friend

ON THE way to the cemetery, tucked into the back seat of the large black limousine belonging to the funeral home, Jane Madison thought to herself: it's a perfect day for a funeral.

And it was—a rainy, dark April day, with the temperature hovering in the high thirties, the New Hampshire hills lost in fog.

Jane's aunt, whom she'd always loved, had finally died after struggling for years with Hodgkin's disease.

As befitted a wealthy woman like Jane's Aunt Sylvia, the burial was in the city's most exclusive cemetery. With its iron gates, carefully terraced and landscaped grounds, and its modern glass-and-wood chapel, the cemetery resembled a country club.

Next to Jane sat her mother, father, and younger brother. Behind them came two long blocks of cars the funeral procession, their headlights on in the rain and gloom.

The minister, out of deference to the weather, kept the graveside ceremony brief.

Jane and her family said their final goodbyes to the woman they'd loved so much.

While she was praying, however, Jane began hearing whispers in her mind.

There was no other way to say it. Somebody invisible seemed to be standing next to her and whispering words and phrases and sentences—but so softly Jane couldn't make sense of what the female voice was saying.

Or was the stress of the funeral simply causing her to imagine things? Jane wondered.

In a few days Jane was back at her normal routine. She worked as a salesperson at a very expensive art gallery in the Loop. She'd majored in art in college and decided this was a good way to put her knowledge to use.

After work, Jane went home to her apartment in Evanston, a suburb of Chicago, and spent the night reading in her lonely apartment. She'd recently broken up with her boyfriend of six years after he'd admitted to regularly having affairs on the side. She was still trying to piece her life back together.

After setting down the book, after trying to get interested in an old black-and-white movie on TV, after washing out lingerie, after fixing herself a ham sandwich that she didn't eat, she sat at the kitchen table, writing a letter to an old college friend. The woman had written Jane seven months ago and Jane was only now getting back to her.

She had written several lines—mostly a long apology for not responding sooner—when she felt her hand begin to move in its own way, as if her own brain impulses were no longer controlling it.

Richard was in love with somebody else.

Her hand had written this very quickly.

All Jane could do was sit there and stare at it.

She had no idea why she'd written it.

She had no idea who Richard was.

What was going on here?

She gripped her fingers around her pen and began writing again.

Could she control her hand this time?

She tried a few words—they were the words she wanted to say.

She tried a few more words. She was back in control again.

She finished her letter to her friend and went to bed, but before sleeping, she lay in the dark a long time thinking about what had happened at the kitchen table tonight.

It was as if some other—being—had suddenly seized control of her hand and had written what *it* wanted to.

But she was being foolish.

She said prayers and counted sheep.

The combination never failed to induce sleep.

A few nights later, Jane was again at the kitchen table again writing a friend a letter, when she again watched her hand write something of its own volition.

Richard betrayed me. That's why I killed myself. He saw his old girlfriend on our wedding day. I know you'll understand.

I contacted you at the cemetery the other day. I know that your boyfriend betrayed you, too.

All Jane could do was sit and stare at the paper.
She knew she wasn't hallucinating.
Pen and paper and words were all very real.
She sat there until it was time for bed.
Her hand wrote no more words.
That night even prayers and counting sheep didn't help.
She was too intrigued by her new adventure to sleep.

Over the next three weeks, Jane had the same experience many times.
She would simply sit down at the kitchen table, pick up the pen—and her hand would begin filling the paper.
Jane had been contacted by a woman named Ruth Foster. The woman had taken her own life in 1946 after her husband, a prominent local politician, had confessed that he had long been unfaithful. Their marriage had undergone many crises like this one—she'd once found him making love to a woman on his office desk—but this time Ruth couldn't deal with it and so killed herself. (Jane learned these things from a realtor who remembered Ruth—and a psychic Jane contacted.)
But because of the circumstances of her death, Ruth was not resting easy in the netherworld.
For one thing, she was lonely, and so when she found Jane at the cemetery, and saw what Jane had been going through, she contacted her through automatic writing.
Jane and Ruth were now good friends.

Their friendship continued. One summer night Jane decided to gather up all the letters Ruth had written and take them to a friend's house.

The friend happened to be a professor of psychology at Northwestern University. He had once been Jane's instructor.

Jane told the man everything that happened and showed him all the letters.

He went through them carefully, looking, as always, interested but skeptical, and finally he said, "You've been very lonely, haven't you, Jane?"

"Lonely?"

"These letters. My dear, don't you see what's going on here?"

"I guess not." Jane had told him of consulting a psychic but the professor only smiled.

"You invented Ruth—she's a perfect friend for you. You've both been betrayed. You've both developed this tragic sense of life. You both feel that nobody really understands you or appreciates you."

He smiled but it was not the sort of smile Jane had wanted to see. This was the smile of an adult for a child who talks incessantly about an imaginary playmate.

"Then you don't believe there's really a Ruth?"

"I think you know the answer to that, Jane."

"But I don't do the writing—Ruth does. Through me."

"Jane, I'm trying to help you. I really am. But I wouldn't be doing you any favors if I simply fed you delusions."

"Delusions?"

"You've been under great stress, Jane. Your relationship ended. Your aunt died. You're lonely and afraid right now."

"So I invented her?"

She wanted to believe what the professor was saying. In a way, it would make things easier.

But she knew better.

There really was a Ruth.

And they really did communicate through automatic writing.

"Maybe you'd like to start seeing me," the professor said.

"Seeing you?"

"Maybe once a week. Just informally. There wouldn't be any fee or anything."

"My God," Jane said, "you're saying I need to see a psychologist."

"Just for a while, Jane. Just until you can deal with your delusion."

Jane wasn't the sort to express her anger at how patronizing the professor was being. She simply found a way to get out of his stuffy little apartment, promising to call him, of course, and then getting in her car and heading home.

The first thing she did was go to the kitchen table, sit down and pick up pen and paper.

He didn't believe you, did he? I could have told you that, Jane. Our friendship has to remain our secret. . . . Other people will simply spoil it by scoffing.

Jane never again mentioned her friend Ruth. Not to anybody but the Society.

Ed Warren

In an introduction to his *Introduction to Psychic Studies*, Hal N. Banks quotes A. Campbell Holms as saying in *The Facts of Psychic Science*:

"Automatic writing is one of the principal means of spirit communication. . . . while writing, the medium usually remains in the normal state, the spirit controlling through the subconscious mind only that part of the brain which moves the hand. . . ."

When the woman we call "Jane" sent her letter to our Society, she went on to say that four decades later, she is still in contact with Ruth through automatic writing.

Jane is now a grandmother many times over, having led a very happy life eventually, but she is a good example of a very normal person who is in constant contact with the realm of the spirits.

Edgar Cayce said that people would benefit from "a natural belief in the supernatural" by which he meant that if people just took the supernatural for granted, as a part of everyday life, they would be much happier and more relaxed.

Jane is a good example of this. She is not particularly interested, her letter states, in any other occult matters, but she does rely on her friendship with her spirit friend Ruth. Her husband and children are well aware of Ruth and are very accepting of her relationship with Jane.

Warning from
a Banshee

THAT SPRING, her life ended. At least, that was how it seemed in retrospect. The time was 1968. The place a small Maine town.

A gifted and very pretty high school teacher of twenty-seven, Ellen Ayles left school late one night, only to find herself confronted by two masked men, who she sensed were actually students of hers.

As soon as one of them grabbed her, she screamed. But it was no use. The only person who might have helped her was the janitor. But as later police investigation proved, he was in the school basement, partaking of a bottle of cheap wine.

Ellen was brutally raped there in the parking lot. She was found, only partially clothed and very badly beaten, wandering down the school alley approximately forty-five minutes after her assailants had fled.

In the coming days, Ellen learned two things: that

some of the medical tests given rape victims are nearly as demeaning as the rape itself; and that many people, including her friends, tended to blame Ellen as much as her assailants.

Why had she walked into a school parking lot after dark by herself? Why didn't she carry a rape whistle? And why wasn't she married by now? The latter question was especially infuriating because, even if she had been married, how could a husband have helped her elude the rapists?

Despite several early breaks in the case, the police were never able to arrest anybody. There just wasn't enough evidence.

Word got around school. Most students were sympathetic. A few, however, found her rape amusing. They left obscene messages on her blackboard and in her locker.

She noticed that even a few teachers seemed to regard her differently now. A few of the female teachers had always been jealous of Ellen. They felt that she used her good looks to get special privileges from the smitten (or so they imagined) assistant principal.

They were not all that unhappy to see her once smiling face set itself into a grim mask. Nor were they unhappy to hear of Ellen inexplicably bursting into tears during a class she was teaching.

That spring, even though the administration was perfectly happy to hire her again, Ellen did not renew her contract. She felt it was time to change her life. She broke up with the man she'd been seeing for the past three years, a breakup painful for both of them. She sold the small house she'd inherited from her father. And she started submitting job applications to school districts where nobody would know her.

• • •

She found a job in Connecticut, in an especially beautiful part of the state where centuries-old buildings had been well preserved and where walking through the rolling hills was a pleasure.

She also found a snug little house to rent. She'd never cared for apartments. At first, she'd had a few misgivings about living this close to a graveyard but then decided she was just being superstitious.

A full year passed. While she could not say she was happy exactly—she felt lonely for her former boyfriend and the rape still troubled her dreams—she did feel much better than she had in the ugly, violent city.

She ate well, jogged a great deal, found a small group of friends who shared her enthusiasm for antiques and began to enjoy her nights alone. In a small town like this, she felt safe.

On the night of April 23, 1974, Ellen went to bed early. She had a headache and felt that she might be getting the same virus that had kept so many students home from school lately.

Later, she would remember waking up and looking at her digital clock. 1:03 A.M.

She was not sure what had awakened her.

Then, barely audible, she heard the wind.

Or at least, that was how she identified the sound—as night wind caught in nearby trees.

She lay in her darkened bedroom, trying to get back to sleep. But she kept listening to the sound. She decided after a while that it wasn't wind.

All she could think of was that a small animal had been injured and was dying painfully somewhere near the house.

She got up, put on her robe, took a flashlight from the storage cupboard and went outside.

The night was cold and sprinkled with raindrops. She felt goosebumps instantly and wished that she'd worn something warmer.

She walked around her small yard, shining her light along the foundation of the house, then searching through the bushes and shrubbery along the perimeter of her yard.

She found nothing.

Nor did she hear the sound.

Whatever it was had ceased.

Two nights later, when she was feeling well enough to stay up for the late movie, she went into the kitchen for a glass of warm milk and there she heard the sound again.

Once more, her first instinct told her that this was the wind. Then she thought of a wounded and dying animal.

She took the flashlight from the cupboard, tugged on her slippers and went outside.

There was a low, almost luminous ground fog. The beam of her flashlight was unable to penetrate most of it.

She spent five minutes looking around. The sound had once again vanished. She found nothing.

She slept very well that night.

On May 6, 1974, Ellen went antiquing with a school friend. They'd stumbled on to a small shop rich with Queen Anne furnishings.

Afterwards, they went for pizza and beer at a small restaurant where teachers hung out.

Ellen, who was not much of a drinker, was home in bed by 11:00.

According to her digital clock, it was 1:27 A.M. when she awoke.

The keening sound was the same as before—yet somehow different, too—more intense.

This time it also sounded very near.

Ellen got up from the bed and went to the bedroom window and saw the young woman for the first time— the woman who seemed composed of fog and mist rather than flesh and blood . . . yet a woman of great beauty . . . and great pain.

Ellen knew this immediately about the apparitionlike figure who stood on the edge of the woods and seemed to beckon to her—the young woman had suffered some terrible tragedy and was trying to share this with Ellen.

Ellen ran to the rocking chair where she always draped her robe. In moments, she was ready to go outside. But this time when she looked through the window—the young woman had vanished. There was only the woods, the trees black and slick after a rain; the dark woods that had always vaguely unsettled Ellen.

She went back to bed but she certainly did not go back to sleep.

"You were going to tell me something, remember?"

Ellen was sitting with her friend Glenda in the teachers' lounge. Glenda had remarked that Ellen looked tired, and Ellen had been about to tell her *why* she looked tired, when the Valentino of higher education, a parody-macho football coach named Jennings, came over and started flirting with Ellen and Glenda. He'd finally left.

In a way, Ellen was glad Jennings had come over. Maybe this wasn't something she should share with somebody. If word got around school. . . .

The bell rang.

Glenda smiled. "The gods don't want me to hear your story."

"Apparently not."

Glenda stared at Ellen a long moment. "You sure you're all right?"

"I'm fine. Just tired."

"Well, if you want to talk about anything, give me a call at home tonight after eight-thirty—you know, when I get the little monsters into their cells."

Glenda had three children. She wasn't exaggerating when she called them "monsters." Ellen had been at Glenda's house before. The three kids were basically out of control. They were going to be outright ogres when they reached their teen years.

"Thanks. Maybe I will give you a call tonight."

After class, Ellen went home and took a nap. She had strange, dark dreams. She was in a deep wood—the woods she'd always imagined when she'd read the Brothers Grimm. She was running toward some-one. . . . A woman was screaming, begging for help. . . .

She came awake slowly. At first she wasn't sure where she was . . . or who she was.

She felt the way she did when she woke up with one of her occasional hangovers . . . trembling and vaguely frightened.

She got up and went into the bathroom and washed up.

She made a roast beef sandwich, opened a small bag of Frito-Lay potato chips, and grabbed a Pepsi. She ate in front of the television, watching the news.

By now, she felt much better.

She remembered telling Glenda that she'd probably call her tonight. By now, it was after 8:30.

She sat in the dark living room, the only light the glow of the TV screen, and talked to Glenda.

They had been gossiping for about ten minutes when Ellen realized she had been paying no attention to the wind that had been gathering outside.

Only when she heard dead leaves slap her window did she look up.

What was going on, anyway? Did New England ever have tornadoes?

"You okay, kiddo?"

"Just this wind. It's really strange."

"Yeah," Glenda said. "Stuff like that spooks me, too."

And then Ellen saw her.

The same spectral figure whom she had seen the other night—the very pretty yet somehow tragic woman who had beckoned to her.

She peered through the French windows, staring at Ellen.

The young woman still appeared to be composed of fog and mist. And she still appeared forlorn.

Then the keening began, the high wailing that had awakened Ellen one night not too long ago.

The young woman raised a slender arm and began waving to Ellen again.

Obviously she wanted Ellen to accompany her. But where? And why?

"Ellen? Is something going on there?"

Ellen had forgotten all about Glenda on the other end of the line.

"I'd better go."

"Something is really wrong there, isn't it?"

"No, Glenda—it's fine."

"You sure you don't want me to call the police?"

"Positive. I appreciate the concern. But everything [is] fine. You're a good friend, Glenda, and I really appre[]ciate it. Goodnight."

Ellen went into the bedroom and pulled on her sho[es] and a heavy winter jacket.

Moments later, she stood at the side of the hous[e] noting that there was no wind except in a small area, th[e] one inhabited by the young woman.

—You must help.

While the women did not speak exactly, she ha[d] somehow managed to communicate words.

It took a few seconds for Ellen to recognize th[e] method being used here—telepathy, one mind speakin[g] directly to another.

—You must help.

—Help with what? Ellen thought.

—She is in trouble.

—Who is in trouble?

—Hurry, the young woman thought. Hurry.

She then led Ellen around to the other side of t[he] house where Ellen's five-year-old Ford sat.

—Hurry. Get in your car. I will lead you.

Ellen sensed the urgency in the young woma[n.] Something terrible was about to happen.

Ellen got in her car, backed out of the narro[w] driveway, and followed the apparition down the win[d]ing road toward town.

Where was she going? What would she find?

Two months earlier, a man named Showalter h[ad] been released from prison, where he'd served a six-ye[ar] sentence for rape. Many had felt that the punishment did not match the crime because in addition to raping a woman, Showalter had also beaten her badly with his fists.

Now, tonight, Showalter waited in some shallow woods on the edge of the Tutwiler Cemetery, waiting for a certain young woman to walk past. She was a waitress and he had been following her for the past two weeks. He knew her schedule very well.

As he stood behind a rain-slicked tree, he felt his entire body tense up. Showalter planned to feel the exquisite pleasure of slamming his fists into the fragile body of a woman.

Down near the curve in the road, headlights picked out the form of a small woman in a raincoat and rain hat making her way up the hill.

Showalter smiled to himself.

The bitch. He was going to show her what pain really meant. He'd watched her smile at the men in the restaurant. She was a quiet, woman, and one who seemed to be both gentle and shy, but he knew what she was really like—a harlot.

And tonight he was going to treat her the way all harlots should be treated.

He waited, his breath coming heavier and heavier.

Soon, soon. . . .

—She is in danger.

—Who?

—You will see her now, very soon.

While Ellen could no longer see her spectral visitor, she heard her very clearly in her mind.

Ellen was now steering the car down the road past the Tutwiler Cemetery.

The road here was slick with rain. She had to b
careful.

She wasn't sure whom she was looking for. Th
specter had mentioned a woman—but where was she

Then Ellen saw her, a small woman, huddled inside
cheap plastic raincoat and hat, picking her way along th
side of the road running past the cemetery.

—You must stop him, Ellen.

Ellen was about to ask who the "him" was when sh
saw a man step out of the trees and move abruptl
toward the woman.

—Stop him, Ellen! Stop him!

Without thinking about what she was doing, Elle
steered the car across the road suddenly, headed righ
for the man.

In her headlights, she could see him throw his hanc
up over his face protectively. His face split open in
scream.

When she was no more than a few inches from him
Ellen slammed on the brakes.

She then leaned over, opened the passenger door an
called to the woman, "Get in! Hurry!"

The woman, who had been standing there lookin
both frightened and confused—first a man appeared ou
of nowhere, then a car crossed the road and nearly ra
him down—now inched toward the door and sai
"Who're you?"

"I'm a friend of yours." Ellen nodded to the man wh
was now retreating back into the woods. "He was goir
to hurt you."

The woman got in the car.

Ellen drove a quarter mile before either said anythin

"How did you know he was there?" the woman sai

"I just knew." Ellen didn't plan on giving any expl

nations. The woman probably wouldn't believe her anyway.

"Do you have to walk home every night?"

"I could take a bus, I suppose," the woman said.

"Then that's what you should do."

The woman stared at her. "He comes into the restaurant where I work. He's always watching me. He gives me the creeps."

"He just got out of prison. He was serving time for raping somebody. And for beating her very badly." Ellen had no idea how she knew this. But somehow the words seemed right and true as she spoke them. "That's what he was planning to do to you tonight."

"I don't understand how you could know all this."

Ellen smiled sadly at the woman. "Neither do I, actually. But what I'm telling you is absolutely true. Now why don't you tell me where you live."

The woman told her.

Ellen drove there, to a shabby part of town even shabbier and lonelier than usual in the rain-washed night.

The woman said, "I owe you a lot."

Ellen shook her head. "I'm just glad you're all right."

The woman smiled. "I'll bet you scared him."

"He deserves to be scared."

"If you're ever by the restaurant, stop in and I'll buy you a cup of coffee."

"That would be nice. Thank you."

The woman got out and walked quickly up the broken walk to her tiny, cabinlike house.

Ellen went home and poured herself a drink and sat in front of the fireplace with a blanket across her legs, reconstructing the night's events.

The waitress had probably thought that Ellen was a kook of some kind.

But Ellen knew better.

Oh, yeah—one look into the man's dark eyes and Ellen had seen it all—all the hatred for women that motivated such men . . . that had motivated her own rapist.

Sometime around midnight, pleasantly intoxicated Ellen's head dropped and she fell asleep.

Two hours later, a knocking woke Ellen.

She came awake, quite sober now, but confused as to the source of the knocking.

Who would be pounding on her door at this late hour?

She got up from the rocking chair and went to the door to check it. By now, the fire had guttered out and the room was filled with long shadows.

"Who's there?" she said, trying the doorknob. She wanted to be sure the door was locked. It was.

No response came. Only the wind.

Suddenly, there was more knocking. She turned around and faced the room.

Empty. No one there to knock.

But there was more knocking immediately.

She stared up at the ceiling.

The sounds seemed to come from overhead.

But that was impossible. There was no upstairs in the small house.

"Who's there?" she called.

But she sensed at once how foolish this was.

Would somebody actually be on her roof, pounding their fists against the shingles?

Of course not!

And then she felt the temperature suddenly drop by many degrees.

Shivering, she went to the rocker, picked up the quilt and wrapped it tight around herself.

More knocking. So furious this time that it seemed to be coming from several places at once.

The temperature got even colder now.

And then right before her, the young woman began to take shape from a swirling, foglike mist in the shadowy corner of the living room.

—I am called Myra. I do not want to frighten you. I am here as your friend, for what happened to you happened to me also. Long ago I was raped in the cemetery one night . . . and then the man dragged me to the deep woods and killed me. That's why I wanted to warn the woman tonight. She is one of our sisters.

And then the woman's form began to flash, alternately light and dark, light and dark.

And then the mist began to swirl again and Myra's features began to fade.

—We are alike, Ellen. Both of us seek vengeance for what was done to us, but it is not likely that either of us will ever have it.

This was simply a voice in Ellen's head. Myra had vanished utterly.

And now even her voice began to fade, as if she were walking down a long hallway . . . and was now beyond Ellen's hearing.

—You have done well, Ellen, and someday you will be rewarded for your kindness.

And then not even the voice could be heard.

The spirit named Myra was gone from Ellen . . . forever.

. . .

Two years later, Ellen met a young doctor, married him, and moved away to St. Louis, where he wished to set up his practice.

Before she left, however, Ellen told her story about Myra to her friend Glenda who, fortunately, had been raised in a household where paranormal phenomena had been discussed openly and rationally.

Indeed, far from scoffing at Ellen's tale, Glenda was quite moved by it. There was a great melancholy attached to this story.

Ed Warren

If you've ever been fortunate enough to spend time in Ireland, you probably know the legend of the banshee—how it always calls on the pure of heart to help those in need.

A friend of ours told us this story one night over dinner. Ellen, it turned out, was his sister, and she had told it to him only many years after the fact.

Our conversation led me to think of a seminar on precognition we'd once given.

Precognition, in case you don't know, means the "ability to perceive and know the future without the aid of sensory clues or inferences" as J. Rhodes Buchanan defined it in *Encyclopedia of Psychic Science*.

A German scientist named Gottmann investigated several dozen cases of "bansheeism" as he came to call it and said that it was really "nothing more than precognition"—a seer warning another human being about something that is going to happen in the future. Gottmann—

et amidst rolling hills with historic headstones, Union Cemetery is pical of the picturesque New England towns that were first settled the early colonial period. It is also haunted. *(Courtesy John Zaffis)*

Ed and Lorraine Warren are standing at the very spot where the ghost of their longtime friend and fellow member of the New England Society for Psychic Research appeared to Ed. *(Courtesy John Zaffis)*

The White Lady is one of the cemetery's most famous ghosts, a remnant of New England's Gothic past who is still occasionally sighted today. It was at this desolate spot that the apparition was filmed walking toward the trees. *(Courtesy John Zaffis)*

This is the historic farmhouse on Sport Hill Road behind Union
Cemetery where the Barberrie brothers lived. It's near the scene
where they first saw the White Lady. *(Courtesy John Zaffis)*

Behind the Baptist Church next to Union Cemetery is a sinkhole where a body was dumped and later mysteriously reappeared at the surface. The trial would become one of New England's most sensational. *(Courtesy John Zaffis)*

It was near this gravestone that the ghost of Ethel Whittaker actually spoke to her old friend Ed Warren. *(Courtesy John Zaffis)*

In the early years of pre-Revolutionary America, churches played a key role in every community. Even today, it is near churches that ghosts are frequently sighted. *(Courtesy John Zaffis)*

This is a rare instance of spirit energy captured on film at Union Cemetery. *(Courtesy Richard Jackson)*

Sean Lorenz, a student of Ed and Lorraine Warren, stands near a gravesite that is shrouded in spirit energy. *(Courtesy Bob Stone)*

Spirit energy sometimes appears on film as a spherical shape. This photograph was taken at Union Cemetery.
(Courtesy Richard Jackson)

this was at the turn of the century—pointed to the young English girl who predicted the exact day World War I would begin—six years before it began. "In effect, then, [Edna Naylor] was a human banshee," Gottmann wrote, "warning the entire world of impending catastrophe. Alas, nobody paid her the least attention."

Speaking
with the Dead

FOLLOWING AN appearance of Ed and Lorraine Warren on "The Larry King Show," the New England Society for Psychic Research received the following letter. The writer asked only that his real name not be used. We think you'll see why.

Dear Ed and Lorraine Warren,

I saw you on television two nights ago and decided that now is the proper time for me to tell my story. Given my position, I'll ask you never to divulge my name. The rest you can use as you see fit.

Following my divorce that September, I said goodbye to Washington, D.C., for a month—I had lived there for sixteen years as a United States senator—and decided to go visit my Aunt Mary in Connecticut. I hadn't wanted the divorce—indeed, had fought against it with a fervor I now find embarrassing—and so I felt in need of a rest.

Two nights before I was to leave, however, I received a late-night phone call from a Dr. Stevenson, who said he had been my aunt's personal physician for many years. "I'm afraid I've got some bad news," he said. "She's dead."

He gave me the details quickly. Aunt Mary, who had been well into her seventies, had died of a heart attack the night before. A neighbor had found her out on the lawn earlier that morning. The doctor had been trying to reach me ever since. Aunt Mary had always talked about me, saying I was the only relative who cared whether she lived or died.

"Do you find it odd that Aunt Mary was out on the front lawn when she died?"

There was a long pause. "Well, sir, I think it's fair to say that your aunt was an odd person. Very warm and very giving—but very odd."

I wanted to ask him more, but he said he had to go. He also said he'd expect to see me in the morning, at which time I could make all the arrangements for the funeral. Then he hung up.

Connecticut was beautiful in the autumn sunlight, the leaves splendidly ablaze, the air warm, the sky blue, and the birch and cedar and maple trees ranked along the clean white fences that lined the road.

Aunt Mary's house was a Tudor that some claimed dated back to the Revolutionary War.

I pulled into the driveway, parked, and carried my three suitcases inside. Aunt Mary had long ago entrusted me with my own key.

Despite the warmth of the fieldstone fireplace and the fine antiques that filled every room, the house felt cold and empty. I didn't have to wonder why. My Aunt Mary, even given her painful arthritis and her sometimes forgetful ways, had always been a cheerful and chattery person. Now there was just the silence.

I walked through the entire house, looking at things that brought back warm memories of my aunt—the loom of which she was so proud, and which she'd operated for me many times; the pewter plates in the china cupboard; the captured British musket that had been my uncle's pride and joy; the heavy, carefully crafted quilts on her canopy bed and on the twin beds in the guest room (at one time, Aunt Mary had even thought of turning her historical house into a bed and breakfast).

It was downstairs in the den that I found the old black stand-up telephone. I hadn't even seen anything like this since I was a very small boy. I remembered visiting here summers with my parents and seeing both my aunt and uncle make all their calls on a phone very much like this one. While such phones had not been used in big cities since the thirties, in rural Connecticut you saw them well into the sixties.

The black phone stood in the middle of a small end table that was covered with a huge white handmade doily. Leaning against the phone was a number ten business envelope with my name—Peter Glendenen — written in my aunt's careful hand across the front of it.

Only when I picked up the envelope did I see that there was no cord coming from the phone. It was not hooked up.

I slid the envelope inside my jacket and left the house.

*Not the real name of this senator.

I was grateful for the warm sunlight. The house had been curiously cold inside.

In town, I found the mortuary and selected a casket for my aunt. She'd been a no-nonsense person and so I bought her a no-nonsense coffin, not much more sophisticated than the venerable pine box. The mortuary man did not look overjoyed.

I next visited the newspaper, the Catholic church, where I arranged for my aunt's services, and finally Dr. Stevenson's office.

The aged medical man was white of hair and dim of gaze. He wore very thick glasses behind which his very blue eyes looked like fish trapped in an aquarium.

He offered me coffee, which I gladly accepted. We spent twenty minutes in his office reminiscing about my aunt. He'd gone to both grade school and high school with her and admitted that he'd had a mad crush on her for many years. But they both married other people and both raised families. Aunt Mary's children, unfortunately for her, had been globetrotters. There were three of them, all grown up now, but only two of them could make it back to the funeral. The third was stranded in Bangkok, which was experiencing some terrible weather.

"You knew her pretty well, did you?" he asked.

"Pretty well. At least I think so."

"Then are you one of her believers?"

"Her believers?"

He leaned forward and put his elbows down on the top of the desk. "One of the people who believe that she was in contact with the spirit world?"

I laughed. "I never thought that was anything except harmless claptrap. I was never sure how seriously Aunt Mary herself took it."

"Very seriously," the old doctor said. "Very seriously."

He seemed about to say more but then his phone rang. I could tell from the way he spoke that one of his patients had a child who was gravely sick. As he finished talking to the caller, he lifted a small leather bag from the floor and set it on the desk.

On the way out of his office, swinging the bag in his left hand and using a gnarled hardwood cane with the other, he reminded me of a New England version of Sherlock Holmes' friend, Dr. Watson.

He climbed into an ancient station wagon and turned on the engine. Before putting the car into gear, he glanced out the window to where I stood by my own car, and said, "Did she say anything about the phone?"

"The phone?"

"Yes. A very old-fashioned phone she kept in the den."

"No. She didn't say anything about it. But if it's the old black one, I've seen it many times over the years."

"According to her, that phone was cursed. She was always telling me stories about it. Crazy stories." He frowned, his jowls settling. "Maybe it'd be best if you'd leave it alone. I don't believe a word of that mumbo jumbo but I guess you can't be positively certain."

He nodded goodbye and left in a cloud of exhaust fumes. I hoped the old medical man took better care of his body than he did of his car.

On the way back to Aunt Mary's, I saw animals of every kind—fox, rabbit, striped skunk, muskrat—and for a city person like me, it was thrilling.

I also passed the Rock of Ages Cemetery. On such a lovely day, even a graveyard was a beautiful spectacle. But I remembered the way Aunt Mary always spoke of the place—in dark and melodramatic terms. "You should never go near there," she'd always warned me. And not just when I was a boy either . . . but well into my adulthood.

I found the refrigerator well-stocked and fixed myself a dinner of bacon, eggs, and thick, jam-covered slices of wheat toast.

I ate on a TV tray in front of Aunt Mary's huge old black and white TV console—huge in frame, that is. The actual dimension of the screen was 17 inches.

After dinner, I fell into a deep sleep. When I awoke, it was night and the countryside was no longer pleasant. A hard autumn rain poured down with jagged lightning cracking across the sky and pale light filling the windows. Sometimes, rain is a pleasant experience; cleansing, soothing. But not this one. This seemed laden with anger and fury.

I carried my dishes into the kitchen, washed and dried them, and then got ready to go upstairs. It was nearing nine o'clock.

In ten minutes, teeth brushed, fresh pajamas on, I slid deep beneath the heavy Yankee quilts covering the old double bed I'd slept in so many times as a boy. I turned the light on and started reading.

I don't recall exactly when I first heard the phone ringing. I just remember being annoyed. Here I was snug and warm in bed with my book.

The prospect of going all the way down there was especially unpleasant with cold rain battering the roof and thunder rumbling across the sky.

But the ringing phone was relentless.

It would stop for a time and then start in again.

Who could be calling, anyway? I wondered.

Finally, I didn't have any choice. I threw back the

quilt, pushed my feet into my slippers, gathered up my robe, and went downstairs.

Not until I was halfway down the winding staircase did I realize how dark the main floor was. For the first time that I could ever recall, I felt a real sense of fear about being in this staid old house. But I laughed it off.

Trying to find a light, I did several variations on the Three Stooges, tripping across an extension cord coiled like a snake beneath a rug, knocking into an end table with a vulnerable knee, and walking head on into a door frame. My favorite Stooge has always been Shemp. He would have been proud of me.

Finally, I found a light and went into the dining room where Aunt Mary had kept her small pink Princess phone sitting on a small antique mahogany lowboy with brass handles and escutcheons.

The phone lay there silent.

Of course—I come all the way down here and the caller decides now is a good time to give up.

Frustrated, I started to walk out of the room. The phone rang.

I turned back to the phone. At least I'd find out who was calling so late and why.

I was halfway to the phone before I realized that the ringing was not coming from this room—but from the room next to it.

But the room next to it was the den where the old-fashioned stand-up phone was. . . . A phone that was not connected to anything.

Real terror gripped me.

What was going on here?

Slowly, reluctantly, I forced myself to go into the next room, where I stood in the doorway staring at the black phone . . .

. . . that rang and rang and rang in the silence.

What choice did I have? I had to go pick it up and find out how a disconnected phone could possibly be ringing.

My mind spun with all sorts of fanciful notions. Maybe with the thunderstorm a phone, even a disconnected one, could receive electrical impulses from the lines strung on the poles outside and. . . .

I grasped the tiny receiver and brought it to my ear.

"Hello?" I said into the mouthpiece.

I have never heard a silence like the one that followed. It was as if I were hearing the silence of outer space itself . . . vast . . . dark . . . unending.

"Hello?" I said again.

I was very conscious now of how vulnerable I was standing in my robe and slippers without any kind of weapon to protect myself.

If anybody or anything were hiding in the house. . . .

"Hello."

But nothing.

And then: "She killed me."

"What?"

"She killed me. Murdered me."

The voice was that of a very young girl—coming from some unimaginable distance.

"She killed me, and two nights ago I showed myself to her and she died. I'm glad she died."

"Who are you?" I asked.

But now there was just that vast unceasing silence once more. I felt goosebumps cover my arms and back.

And then that very special silence was no more.

I was just a very silly man holding a disconnected phone in his hand.

Then, I glanced at my sport coat hanging on the back

of a chair in the kitchen. I'd forgotten all about the letter Aunt Mary had left me.

I took it and went back to the den where I turned on a Tiffany bronze lamp that Aunt Mary had been especially fond of.

And then I read her letter.

Dear Peter,

You're the only member of my family—including my own children—who ever had any special affection for me. Not even your own mother cared for me, her own sister, all that much.

So it is to you that I'll address this story. You may choose to believe it or not.

When I was eighteen years old, I bore a child out of wedlock. Because I never looked in the "family way," nobody ever knew I was pregnant.

On the chill, rainy night of the infant's birth—which took place in my father's barn—I took the infant girl to Rock of Ages Cemetery and killed her. I buried her in a shallow grave next to the headstones belonging to five generations of our family.

A year later, I met a respectable young man and married him. Your uncle was a wonderful man—giving, caring, sensitive. He deserved a better mate than me, for by then I had given my life over to matters of the occult and nothing else mattered to me.

And why the occult?

For a while I had managed to make my peace with what I'd done to that infant girl. But one night, just as I was turning twenty-eight years old, the phone rang downstairs in the middle of the night . . . the very same phone that sits now in the den.

Your uncle being a heavy sleeper, I went down and answered the phone and heard for the first time the voice of the baby girl I'd killed.

Or was it really her?

Somebody could have found out what I'd done and begun to taunt me with it. . . .

But no. I knew in my heart that the girl was contacting me from beyond the grave.

She hated me . . . and I well understood why.

The rest of my life passed far too quickly. I went about the world trying to learn more about the supernatural. I wanted to learn some way to make my tiny daughter forgive me.

She called at will and at random over the years.

I watched my family grow up to be strong and independent young men and women . . . and I watched the ravages of heart disease take your uncle.

Soon I was a widow . . . alone in the old house . . . and at the mercy of the phone calls.

A month ago, she told me that she would show herself to me some night . . . show herself to me as she looked after I plunged a kitchen knife deep into her infant chest.

I have no doubt that she is telling the truth, Peter. One night I will look out on my lawn and see her and—

I know it will kill me. I will die of a heart attack just as my husband did.

But do I deserve any less punishment, Peter? After what I did, can there ever be any forgiveness?

Love,
Aunt Mary

I sat up late into the night reading and rereading the letter in my lap.

Thunder roared and rumbled; lightning flickered and flashed. And the rain, cold and sodden, beat without end or mercy.

Every few minutes, I would look over at the old-fashioned black phone and remember that small, sad little girl's voice I'd heard earlier in the evening.

I had no doubt that my aunt's letter was absolutely true.

In the morning, no longer caring to be a part of this house or its history, I packed my things and returned to the city.

Lorraine Warren

Following World War II, the Soviet Union spent a good deal of time and money investigating various kinds of ESP. It was whispered, though never confirmed, that Stalin had once had some sort of contact with a dead relative. Apparently, Stalin considered this a form of telepathy, a subject he was very interested in.

In Russia, such men as Dr. Nikolai Semyonov, who had won a Nobel prize in chemistry, and Dr. Gleb Frank, a brilliant educator, also expressed a similar interest in the subject.

Intensive investigations were launched. Previously unspeakable subjects were spoken of openly—not only telepathy but genuinely occult topics such as conversing with the dead.

There's no doubt that the man who wrote us truly had the experience he thinks he did. He indeed communicated with the dead girl. This is another example of an unsettled spirit needing to share her feelings with a living being.

Today the man lives in New York and works as an administrator for the public school system. He has remarried.

The Dead
Return to Earth

Prom night, 1958. The Bevins sisters, very pretty young girls, were getting ready. Sandy Bevins was a junior, Katy Bevins a senior. Their dates were the captain and co-captain of the football team.

All was idyllic until Katy Bevins decided to go for a quick walk before their dates were to arrive.

The early Rhode Island dusk was rainy. The road Katy took was covered with fallen autumn leaves. She wore her brother's old P-coat, bundled up inside it. Occasionally, headlights flashed then died in the darkness, leaving her to the lonely road.

The truth was, Katy was having the dreams again. Two months earlier she'd picked up a newsstand magazine devoted solely to ghosts and ghouls. From reading a dozen or so articles, she'd learned that some people really did contact the dead.

When Katy was eight, she lost her best friend Donna

to a freak schoolyard accident. Katy and Donna had been playing on top of the jungle gym. Katy had given Donna a playful push. Donna lost her grip, screamed, and fell to the ground.

She landed directly on her head, snapping her neck in the process.

Katy knew instantly that Donna was dead. The way her left arm and right leg were so twisted . . . the way her head was at such a severe angle to her neck. . . .

Several girls had gathered around to see what had happened to their little friend on this warm spring afternoon.

One of the girls crawled through the jungle gym and went over to Donna.

Katy couldn't move. Sick, terrified, all she could do was stare down at Donna in cold horror.

The girl who'd come to help Donna started screaming. Two girls ran to get a teacher.

Even when the teacher returned, even when she lifted the small, broken body and carried it over to the grass, even when some of the other girls stood staring up at her—not even then could Katy move. All she could think of was giving Donna that playful shove. . . .

At the funeral, Donna's mother walked past Katy and her parents without saying a word. Katy had told her teacher all about playfully pushing Donna. Obviously, Donna's mother held Katy responsible for her daughter's death.

The woman never again spoke to Katy. Within six months of the funeral, Donna's family left the area and did not return.

By age twelve, Katy was a true beauty. With lovely dark hair and blue eyes, she had a supple body, and was the girl all other girls measured themselves against.

Most girls would have taken advantage of such good looks. Not Katy. She was shy and remote, which got her the reputation of being stuck-up; and she was a straight-A student, which got her the reputation of feeling superior to her friends.

But she was neither, as her parents' monthly checks to a local psychologist proved. Katy had never gotten over her guilt for playing a role in Donna's death. She needed to see a psychologist constantly . . . or fall into one of her frightening periods of withdrawal. During one of these periods, she'd stayed in her room for three weeks, refusing to talk or eat. She was a slender girl by nature. After three weeks of fasting, she looked gravely ill.

In all, Katy saw the psychologist for more than seven years. For a working-class family such as hers, the bills were backbreaking. But her father insisted that she keep on seeing the psychologist. He was afraid of what might happen to his daughter otherwise.

Besides Dr. Fenwick, only walking seemed to lift her spirits. She would get up at dawn some mornings and walk all day. She loved the Rhode Island countryside. She would read an article or book about a certain site and then go visit it.

For most of her life she had been aware of Telfair Cemetery. On sunny days, she found the place oddly beautiful. On rainy or snowy days, she found that the place had a certain dignity.

This was Katy's life and frame of mind two months before the prom . . . on the day, quite by chance, she stopped into the drugstore for some lipstick, bought a cherry fountain Coke, and sat gazing at the magazine stand.

The occult magazine stood out. Despite the clutter of

all the other magazines, this one alone attracted her attention.

She went over and picked it up, planning only to skim through it while she finished her Coke.

But as soon as she opened the cover, she found herself enraptured.

Ever since Donna's death, Katy had been looking for some way to put her life back together.

She needed to have Donna's forgiveness.

And what better way to seek that forgiveness than by talking to Donna on the other side?

She quickly paid for the magazine and strolled out into the warm autumn day.

She walked down the street, bumping into people but scarcely noticing.

She just kept turning pages, studying the text intently.

She was reading about a young New Jersey girl who had daily visited a cemetery . . . and in so doing had contacted the spirit of her younger sister.

This was how she'd reach Donna!

This was perfect!

Over the next five weeks, while everybody in the family was talking about how nice it would be that Katy and Sandy would be double-dating at the prom (almost as corny as a Hailey Mills identical-twins movie)— while everybody else was having a good time getting ready for the prom, Katy was becoming an obsessed student of the occult.

She spent hours in the library and in dusty used bookstores trying to find every book possible on the subject of communicating with the dead.

Her parents were aware of Katy's new passion, and while they were not happy about it, what could they do? Despite her beauty and brains, she had always been a strange girl . . . and wasn't likely to change.

Now when Katy went for walks, it was straight to Telfair Cemetery. No more tours of the countryside. No more visits to quaint covered bridges.

She spent hours in the graveyard, using every method she'd found in the books to contact the dead girl. Even though Donna had been buried elsewhere, Katy knew she could contact her here . . . if only she were patient.

But not until the night of the prom did Katy have any luck.

Unfortunately, it was not good luck at all . . .

The theme of the prom was the familiar "Stairway to the Stars." Even some of the homely girls looked lovely in their gowns and corsages, and even a few of the gawkier boys seemed to have learned some self-control and poise for this occasion.

A five-piece band played the day's favorite tunes, everything from rock-and-roll to Tony Bennett ballads.

Teachers hovered near the punch bowl, making certain that nobody spiked it, while the janitor walked around the perimeter of the red brick high school, looking for anybody who might have a flask.

The Bevins girls sat with their dates at a small table near the bandstand. At one point they each changed dates for one dance.

Midway through the ceremony, the king and queen were crowned. Many thought that Katy should be queen, but her reputation for aloofness kept some students from voting for her.

After the dance their dates took them to a fashionable

restaurant where both boys tried, without any luck, to buy liquor with false IDs.

The waiter laughed. "You boys are too well-known to try and fool me."

Katy and her sister laughed, too.

The girls had been told to be in by midnight and no later. While their folks were "liberal" by some standards, they were absolute about curfew.

On the way back home, Sandy got into a heavy necking session in the backseat.

Katy smiled. Sandy was so much more "modern" than Katy was. In some ways, Katy envied her. Tonight, for example, Katy would let herself be kissed a few times before going inside . . . but that would be all.

She'd been out one night with a boy who'd managed to insinuate his hand up under her blouse while they were kissing. She'd slapped him and insisted on walking home from the drive-in theater where he'd taken her.

On the way home, all she'd been able to think about was that she was not entitled to have fun . . . not when Donna couldn't have any fun, either.

The car was just passing by Telfair Cemetery, when Katy saw the little girl.

She screamed.

Tru, her date, slammed on the brakes.

Sandy sat up in the backseat, saying, "What's wrong, Sis?"

"That little girl," Katy said.

"What little girl, Sis?"

"The one I just saw on the road there. Didn't you see her, Tru?"

"Huh-uh. Sorry."

"But she was right out in plain sight, right on the edge of the road."

Tru shrugged. "I didn't see her, Katy. Honest."

Sandy knew the significance of the "little girl" Katy had claimed to see. At least two or three times a month, Katy was sure she saw her friend Donna. This was one of the reasons that Katy kept on seeing her psychologist.

Tru started driving again.

Katy stared out the window at the dark, rain-chilled night and the headstones of the cemetery.

She had seen a little girl, the same little girl she often saw.

And she knew who the little girl was, too. Donna, of course.

All Katy's work had paid off. She'd finally made contact with the young friend she'd killed.

She would have a talk with Donna, and Donna would forgive her.

Tru kissed Katy twice at the door. Sandy and Bob were still in the car.

"I guess you know how much I like you," Tru said.

For a popular kid, football hero, and owner of a magnificent singing voice, Tru was incredibly shy.

Katy felt sorry for him. She wished she liked him more. Wished she could give him some encouragement.

"I'd like to see you again," Tru said.

But thankfully, before Katy even had time to think of something gentle to say, the door opened and there was Dad.

"You kids have a good time?"

"Great time, Mr. Bevins," Tru said, and then nodded goodnight and walked down the steps to the car.

"How about that sister of yours," Dad said. "Think she's planning on coming in tonight?"

Katy grinned. She liked it when her dad, who could be a pretty gruff guy, teased the girls.

"You have a nice time tonight, kiddo?"

"Uh-huh. Tru's a nice kid."

"It isn't hard to see that you make his little heart go pitter-pat."

She laughed, embarrassed.

"And something else happened, too," Katy said.

"Oh?"

"On the way past the graveyard—"

She saw her dad tense, knowing what was coming. "—I saw Donna."

Right there in the doorway, he took her in his arms and held her tight. She could tell he was ready to cry again, the way he'd cried the first time she told him that she went to the graveyard so she could talk to her friend.

"Oh, darlin'," he said, "can't you forget about Donna? How many times do I have to tell you, it wasn't your fault what happened. It was just an accident, a terrible accident."

"But I pushed her, Dad. She wouldn't be dead if I hadn't pushed her."

He still held her tight. "You were only playin', Katy. That's all. Playin'."

An hour later, Katy was in her room, tucked deep into her bed.

And wide awake.

She'd tried all the usual means of getting to sleep—warm milk, counting sheep, closing her eyes and saying prayers—yet nothing worked.

She was awake . . . and thinking about the little girl she'd seen on the road next to Telfair Cemetery.

Why hadn't Tru seen the girl? Was she losing her mind? She had recently read an article on psychosis and knew that some people actually believed they saw monsters and aliens from outer space.

How about little girls who had been dead for several years?

Was that simply her imagination?

The house was silent and dark when she left it forty-three minutes later.

The night was cold and the road leading to the cemetery empty.

She huddled inside her long winter coat, put her head down and walked as quickly as possible.

By the time she reached the graveyard, she was excited. She knew she would see her old friend tonight.

She went to one of the large headstones on the edge of the place and began calling Donna's name.

At first, all she heard was the dark night—the wailing wind, the patter of light rain on the sodden ground, the distant roar of traffic.

"Donna, please talk to me. I saw you earlier tonight. I know I did."

Nothing.

Now she closed her eyes, as if in prayer. She thought of all the incantations she'd read about, all the strange words for summoning up the dead she'd memorized over the past few months.

And then a voice said, "Katy. You killed me, Katy."

And when Katy opened her eyes, only a few feet away, stood the glowing form of a young girl dressed in jeans and a blouse, her hair done in pigtails the way

Donna's had always been. A curious yellow light surrounded the girl, seeming to radiate from somewhere on her body. The glow enclosed the little girl.

Then Katy noticed the girl's face.

The skin had been ravaged by some kind of disease, the flesh eaten away in places. All Katy could think of was lepers and leprosy, which she had studied in school.

The girl put her hand out for Katy to touch.

Large sores showed on the skin.

Katy did not want to touch this hand.

"Who are you?" she managed to say.

The young girl smiled. But the expression was not friendly. There was hatred in it. "I'm your friend Donna. The friend you killed, remember?"

"You're not Donna. You don't look anything like Donna."

The girl lunged at Katy, grabbing the sleeve of her coat and ripping it from the shoulder.

Katy screamed.

The little girl began circling her.

Whenever Katy tried to move, the girl moved, too, blocking her way.

The girl lashed out again, grabbing the other sleeve and ripping it away.

"You're going to look just like me in a little while!" the girl cried out at one point.

Katy looked desperately around the graveyard for some means of escape.

Her only hope, she saw, was to run between two large headstones behind her and try to reach the road.

As the little girl moved closer and closer to her, she continued to radiate the peculiar yellow light.

"You called me, Katy," she said. "And now you're going to be my friend."

The girl's voice had become lower now, almost as if a man were lurking inside the girl's body.

Katy turned and ran.

She reached the two large headstones quickly and started to turn right, toward the road.

And that was when the girl jumped on Katy's back, knocking her to the ground.

Katy struggled to get out from under the little girl but it was impossible.

Lying on her stomach, she kept kicking and flailing her arms as best she could, even bucking and trying to throw the girl off. Katy felt her entire coat become soaked with some kind of hot, puslike material that dripped from the girl's body. Katy had never felt more unclean in her life.

The girl yanked and tugged on Katy's hair so hard that Katy started screaming.

Then the girl jumped from Katy's back and ran around front and said, "You killed Donna! You killed your best friend!"

As Katy was struggling to her feet, the glowing girl jumped on her and seized her throat, starting to strangle her immediately.

The stench was terrible. Up close, the girl was even more hideous, the leperlike sores oozing green fluids, the eyes a crimson color.

The girl choked her harder . . . harder . . . until Katy felt herself begin to sink into total darkness. . . .

She heard her own screams. . . .

Felt her fists clench and unclench. . . .

And then somewhere, faintly, she heard someone shouting her name.

"Katy! Katy!"

And then all was darkness. . . .

• • •

Six hours later, Katy opened her eyes to see her parents and her sister standing over her. They were smiling.

"You're all right now, hon," her mother said.

"Thanks to your sister," Dad said.

Sandy smiled. "I heard you get up last night, and I got worried about you. When I heard you go out the door, I put my coat over my pajamas and went after you. I figured you were headed for the graveyard and that's where I found you."

Katy thought back to last night. The walk to the cemetery. The little girl. The strange glow. The terrible odor. The strangling.

Katy said, "Did you see her?"

Sandy looked at her parents before answering. "See who, Katy?"

"The little girl."

"Donna, you mean?"

"No, it wasn't Donna. It was—a different little girl."

Sandy looked at her parents again. The smiles were gone. They were concerned.

"I'm afraid the only person I saw there was you, Katy."

"But there was a little girl. There was a glow all around her. She was strangling me and—"

Then she quit talking, knowing how insane she must sound. Glowing little girls in midnight grave yards. . . .

"Dr. Fenwick is coming to see you," Mom said.

"Here?"

She smiled. "He said he needed a break from his office routine so he thought he'd drop by and see how you were doing."

Katy had never heard of psychologists who made house calls. . . .

And then Katy scratched her lower right forearm. It had been itching ever since she awakened a few minutes earlier.

She pushed up the sleeve of her pajamas and stared at a small green oval several inches below the crook in her elbow.

The oval was rough to the touch—all she could think of was some kind of lizard skin—and it was faintly warm, too.

"What's that?" Dad said.

Katy shook her head. "I don't know."

"Let's have a closer look at it," Mom said.

Mom and Dad spent the next twenty minutes examining the oval. They'd never seen anything like it.

"Does it hurt, hon?" Mom said.

"Huh-uh."

"Does it burn?"

"Not really."

"And you didn't notice it until this morning?"

"It's from the little girl. I mean, I know you don't believe that I actually saw her but I did. This mark is from her."

Dad glanced at Mom. Katy could tell that they were beginning to believe her story at least a little bit.

Dr. Fenwick spent twenty minutes talking with Katy.

"Describe her to me, this little girl."

So Katy described her.

"And you think she intended to kill you?"

"I know she did. And she would have if Sandy hadn't shown up to help me."

"But Sandy didn't see her?"

"No."

"And earlier in the evening, Tru didn't see her, either?"

"No." Katy paused. "You don't believe me, do you?"

"I believe that you believe every word you're telling me."

"That isn't the same thing as believing me, though, is it?"

"I guess it isn't, is it, Katy?"

"I want you to look at something."

"All right."

By now, Katy was dressed in jeans and a sweater. She pushed up the arm on her sweater and showed the odd green mark to the good doctor.

Or tried to.

The mark wasn't there any longer.

The skin looked white and completely normal.

No evidence whatsoever that a curious green oval with a very rough surface had ever been there.

"It was there. Right there."

"Tell me about it."

She told him about it.

"Mom and Dad and Sandy all saw it."

"They did?" He looked and sounded surprised.

The psychologist spent his final twenty minutes with Katy's parents. He emerged looking puzzled. He was convinced that the little girl was completely imaginary . . . but then how could he explain the green mark on Katy's skin? What was that all about?

Over the next six weeks, Katy's parents began to take her story much more seriously. They had seen the green mark, they could tell that it was not of natural origin, and they wanted some real help from somebody who understood what was happening to their elder daughter.

Through a parish priest, Katy's parents learned of a woman knowledgeable about the occult and invited her to speak with Katy.

The woman recognized the problem immediately and set about giving Katy the correct advice.

Ed Warren

The other night, Lorraine and I were watching a sit-com we usually enjoy. But this particular episode alarmed us.

One of the regulars on the show, a teenage girl, found an old Ouija board in the attic, brought it downstairs and began playing with it.

The plot had the girl get her little brother to join her in "trying to contact the spirit world."

Well, the show degenerated into standard sit-com silliness (we watch such shows to relax after long hard days—the same reason millions of other Americans also watch). The girl couldn't sleep, stayed up into the wee hours playing with the board in her bedroom . . . and her little brother jumped out of the closet to scare her.

Ouija boards are just as dangerous as drugs. They're not to be played with.

When we heard about the Bevins sisters, we saw yet another example of teenagers literally inviting supernatural problems into their lives.

Just as parents are responsible for other aspects of their children's lives, they should take equal care to keep the tools of the devil from their children . . . especially in an era when satanic cults are on the rise.

Remember: Seances and Ouija boards and other occult paraphernalia are dangerous because evil spirits often disguise themselves as your loved ones—and take over your life.

The Man
Who Was Two

ON THE morning of March 14, 1988, a chemical engineer from Bangor named Scott Weybright sat on the edge of his bed, rubbing his face and trying to forget the dream he'd had again last night.

The dream that was slowly turning into a nightmare.

After shaving, showering, dressing in suit and tie for the day, Scott went downstairs where, as usual, his wife Carol had breakfast ready for him.

Carol was a slender blonde, even prettier at thirty-five than she'd been at twenty-five.

She served him a poached egg, two pieces of toast, two vitamin C capsules, and a cup of steaming coffee.

Scott sat in the breakfast nook, glumly staring out at the sunny, springlike day.

"The dream again?"

"Uh-huh," he said. And then turned to face her.

He could tell by her small gasp of surprise how bad he looked. He hadn't had a good night's sleep in two weeks.

He sipped coffee. "I remember we were going to move out to the suburbs so we could get some peace and quiet." He shook his head. "I guess it hasn't worked out that way."

The Weybrights had lived in an apartment until three months ago when Scott had been promoted to head of his department. At last they'd been able to afford a house. Carol had spent all her time house-hunting. They'd found this nice suburban house empty and moved right away.

Two nights later, Scott had the dream the first time.

Now, Scott tried to eat but couldn't. He'd lost four pounds in the past week.

"Try putting a little jam on the toast," Carol said softly.

"The old sweet-tooth routine, eh?" Scott tried to sound humorous. But he was too tense to be humorous.

"Why don't you let me call Dr. Goodman?" she said.

"What if he says I'm crazy—schizoid or something?"

"Honey, you're not crazy. This dream has to do with stress. I'm sure of it. You have a lot more responsibility at work and a much bigger mortgage to meet every month. That's all the dream is about—how you feel boxed in by all your obligations." She reached over and touched his hand. "Please let me call Dr. Goodman. Please?"

She had been asking him this for the past eight mornings.

This particular morning, he did not say no.

"Let's go back through the dream once again," Dr Goodman said. A heavyset man with graying hair

Goodman was a celebrated psychotherapist, head of the New York State Association of Psychotherapists, and a man who frequently appeared on national talk shows.

Early in their marriage, Carol and Scott had had some problems, Scott feeling confined. In his time and in his way, he'd been something of a ladies' man. He'd found marriage suffocating in some ways.

After seeing Dr. Goodman on TV, Carol had phoned his office. Dr. Goodman began seeing the couple. Within six visits, the Weybright marriage was sound again.

"You mean tell you the whole thing?"

"If you don't mind, Scott."

Late afternoon shadows collected in the corners of his fern-filled office with its wall of books, large, very tidy desk, and its two leather armchairs that sat facing each other for doctor and patient respectively.

"Well," Scott began, "it's late at night. Something wakes me up but I'm not sure what. I get up from bed and start walking down the hall. I go down the stairs to the main floor and then I go to the kitchen. I walk over to the counter and open a drawer and take out this huge butcher knife. Then I go back upstairs. It's very dark in our bedroom. And hot. Every time it's hot, as if the thermostat broke and it's over a hundred degrees. I can feel myself sweating but it's a cold sweat. Very cold. I look over at the bed and Carol is sleeping very peacefully. I can hear her breathing—very regular and soft. She's perfectly peaceful. And then all of a sudden some impulse overcomes me, and I rush to the bed and kneel next to her and raise the knife so I can stab her in the chest and—"

He stopped. "And then I always wake up."

"So you don't actually stab her?"

"No. But I'm certainly ready to."

Dr. Goodman of the gray hair and the black horn-rimmed glasses and the good Brooks Brothers tweed sport coat with the leather patches—Dr. Goodman nods. "You're right, Scott. That's a very disturbing dream."

"Does it mean that I want to kill Carol?"

"No, not at all. But it does mean you're frustrated—or afraid. When I was seeing both you and Carol, it was obvious that commitments frightened you. You couldn't decide if you loved Carol enough to stay married. Now, I think, with the new job and the house you're starting to feel suffocated again. That's what your dream is about. The suffocation we all feel when we think we're overcommitted."

Scott smiled. "Actually, I could have stayed home today. That's exactly what Carol said at breakfast the other day."

"Carol's very perceptive."

"Then you don't think that deep down I want to kill Carol?"

"No, I don't."

Scott felt ecstatic. He was going to go home, sweep Carol up in his arms, and then take her out to some place fancy for dinner.

"But I would like to talk to you today about dealing with commitments, Scott."

"Fine," Scott smiled. "Let's talk."

The next seven days were good ones.

The dream came no more. Scott and Carol enjoyed a kind of second honeymoon, going to the ballet (Carol's choice), a boxing match (Scott's choice), and several movies they'd been meaning to see. And their appetites went international as they dined at Italian, Chinese, Greek, and Indian restaurants.

On the eighth night the dream was back again. Only this time, it wasn't a dream. . . .

At 2:43 A.M. the Weybright kitchen was shadowy and silent except for the hum of the refrigerator and the occasional wind rapping on the windows.

Scott Weybright stood in the center of the kitchen, bare feet on cold tiles, clad only in pajama bottoms. His body was icy with sweat. In his right hand he gripped the handle of the butcher knife.

Or was this a dream?

But no. Just then a drop of water fell from the faucet and *tocked* against the sink.

And the wind rattled the windows.

No; this was no dream.

He started walking.

Out of the kitchen. Through the dining room. To the staircase.

Up the stairs, carpet nubby against the soles of his feet.

Higher; higher. Reaching the second floor landing.

Turning right . . . toward the bedroom where Carol slept so peacefully.

Into the bedroom and—

Slower now—

Breath coming in hot surges that burned his lungs and throat—

As he drew closer to the bed; closer—

He leaned over, raising the knife as he did so.

He started bringing the knife down and then—

His cry woke Carol instantly.

When she got a light on, she found her husband

huddled in the corner, the butcher knife lying a few feet from him.

She hurried to him, tried to speak but saw that it would do no good. He was in shock of some kind.

She stood up and walked quickly down the hall to the den.

She clipped on the light, found the emergency number for Dr. Goodman, and called him.

Two weeks later, on the morning of May 6, 1988, Dr. Goodman opened his office door and said to Scott Weybright, "Come in, Scott, I'd like you to meet Tina Burns."

Burns was an attractive woman in her early forties. She wore a green knit dress that flattered her red hair and green eyes.

Scott shook Tina's hand, Dr. Goodman pulled up an extra chair, and the three sat down.

"Are you familiar with the word 'parapsychologist,' Scott?"

"People who investigate occult activities, you mean?"

"Something like that, yes," Goodman said. "Given all the trouble you've been having lately, I thought I'd call Tina in and get her feelings about what's going on out at your house."

"I'm surprised you believe in things like this," Scott said.

"Well, I may not be as skeptical as I appear," Dr. Goodman smiled. "And Tina has helped me with several of my patients."

Goodman stood up. "Now I'll leave you alone. I'm going down to the corner for a cup of coffee and I'll be back in an hour or so."

Tina and Scott said goodbye.

· · ·

"Have you been hearing voices, Scott?"

"I'm not insane, if that's what you mean."

"No need to get defensive, Scott. I'm merely trying to help you."

"All right." He paused. "Yes, I have been hearing voices—or rather, a voice."

"Does it have a sex?"

"Male. Middle-aged, I'd say."

"Speaks English?"

"Yes." He smiled. "Or I wouldn't be able to understand it."

"No accent, I meant."

"No, no accent."

"What does the voice say?"

Scott thought a moment. "It urges me to kill Carol."

"As in the dream?"

"Yes, to go downstairs and get the butcher knife and come back upstairs and stab her in her sleep."

"Did you hear the voice the other night when you awoke in the kitchen?"

"Yes—or I thought I did, anyway. But just for a moment."

"Does the voice say anything else?"

"Sometimes it mentions a woman."

"Does the woman have a name?"

"Norma."

"A last name?"

"Not that I remember."

"Does it ever say anything about this Norma?" Tina asked.

"Once it said, 'She'll betray you just like Norma betrayed me.'"

"You're sure?"

"Yes, because it got scary, hearing how angry the voice was."

"Anything else?"

He shrugged. "It just keeps telling me to kill Carol." He stared at Tina. "I don't want Carol to know that I hear this voice. That's why I haven't even told Dr. Goodman."

"You're afraid they'll think you're insane?"

"Right."

"I'll need a few days, Scott."

"A few days?"

"To look into this."

"You really think you can help?"

"Let's say I hope I can," Tina smiled.

At dinner that night, when Carol asked Scott about his session with Dr. Goodman, he didn't tell her about Tina or about their conversation.

"It went very well," was all he said.

"Do you feel any better?"

"I'm getting there. Little by little."

Carol had prepared a candle-lit meal, hoping that the romantic atmosphere might calm Scott.

"You can sleep in our bed tonight if you want to," Carol said softly.

"Not yet. I still want you to sleep alone and to lock the door from the inside."

"But, Scott—"

"I just don't trust myself, Carol. After the other night—"

Carol sighed. "I love you, Scott. I hope you know that."

"I know that, Carol, and I appreciate it. Right now it's the only thing that's keeping me going."

They had more wine and spoke of other, pleasanter topics.

Tina had been trained by the New England Society for Psychic Research.

Using its methods, she immediately went to the city clerk's office and began investigating the history of the Weybright house, when it had been built and—more important—what had occupied the land before the house had been built there.

At first, she found nothing that was very useful but then one of the older clerks remembered something about the neighborhood and said, "Let me go back even before 1930. Let's see what we find."

He was an older man with white hair and a spiffy red bow tie. Tina had made sure to flatter him. Even at his age, he was susceptible to flattery.

The clerk spent the next half hour digging through books.

Finally he reappeared and said, "Got somethin' here you might be interested in, young lady."

At age 43, Tina loved the idea of somebody calling her "young lady." She, too, was susceptible to flattery.

Four days later, once again in Dr. Goodman's office, Tina sat across from Scott Weybright.

She said, "In 1928 a man named Rollins murdered his wife, whom he believed had been unfaithful to him. He stabbed her to death. Her name was Norma. Sound familiar?"

"Very familiar."

"I thought it might. Anyway, after killing her and wrapping her in a tarpaulin, Rollins went into a panic. What was he going to do? Well, he ran his own home construction company so he thought of hiding her in the foundations on one of his houses. He thought this was very clever because, before he'd started building homes on it, this land had been a cemetery.

"He took her out there and dug a shallow grave in the soil where the foundation would go and then he went home to wait until morning when he called the police to say that his wife was missing.

"Well, Rollins was a very violent man. He'd been arrested any number of times for drunk and disorderly, so naturally when he reported his wife missing, the police were suspicious.

"They staked his house out and started following him everywhere he went.

"And one place he couldn't resist going was the construction site where he'd buried his wife.

"He drove out there six, seven times a day—and several times a night. This went on for nearly a week. Finally the police got suspicious. Why was he always driving past that construction site?

"Then one night Rollins got out of the car and went over to where he'd buried his wife. He started talking to her, the way some people talk to graves in a cemetery.

"He was saying vile things to his wife. He was also saying that he was happy he killed her.

"Well, the police officer crept up behind him and told him to put his hands up, but Rollins being the violent man that he was, pulled a gun from his pocket and shot the police officer in the chest.

"But before the policeman fell, he put three bullets in Rollins, who fell down right on top of the grave he'd dug for his wife . . . and died.

"Ironically, the policeman lived. He told investigators everything he'd learned and the case was closed."

"So it's Rollins's spirit that was trying to get me to kill Carol?"

"Exactly."

"Is there anything we can do?"

"An exorcism."

"Really?"

"Really."

"I thought that was just in the movies."

Tina laughed. "Not anymore."

On June 2, 1988, an exorcism was performed at 2437 Robincrest Lane.

Present were Scott and Carol Weybright, Tina Burns, and a Catholic priest named Father Flaherty.

The ceremony took two-and-a-half hours. During the course of it, the neighbors heard shrieking of an ungodly sort—and "ungodly" was the right term.

Rollins, who was now a demon, shrieked and cursed until he was finally driven out entirely.

2437 Robincrest Lane is today a happy home.

Scott and Carol have two children and a very loving and supportive marriage.

And they never forget to send Tina Burns a Christmas card.

Lorraine Warren

Several years after this took place, Tina told us that Scott Weybright had become such a convert to parapsychology that he told anybody who would listen of his experience.

Given the fact that most of his co-workers and virtually all of his friends were scientists, Scott's words and enthusiasm earned him a reputation for being somewhat "eccentric." "What they're really saying," Scott laughingly told Tina one day, "is that I'm nuts."

Then one day, while reading Hal N. Banks's *Introduction to Psychic Studies*, Scott came across a quote from famed scientist William James, who noted:

"Why do so few 'scientists' ever look at the evidence for telepathy, so called? Because they think, as a leading biologist, now dead, once said to me, that even if such a thing were true, scientists ought to band together to keep it suppressed and concealed. It would undo the uniformity of nature and all sorts of other things without which scientists cannot carry on their pursuits. . . ."

Ed and I love to quote this to our scientific friends. It keeps them humble.

My Grandfather,
the Monster

ONE GRAY and rainy day in 1946, a ten-year-old Susan Daily climbed the stairs to the attic and saw something that would change her life forever.

The house Susan lived in was large and boxy and white. Because of the heating bills, Susan's parents kept the attic door closed. But sometimes Susan took one of her Nancy Drew books up there to read. She liked sitting in the comfortable old rocker that had belonged to her great-grandmother, and she liked looking out the dusty window to the yard below. She sometimes pretended that she was a princess and that all the land below was her realm, to rule as she saw fit.

She opened the attic door now and began climbing. The stairs were steep and many times she was winded before she reached the top.

Even when it was sunny, the attic was a shadowy and somber place. She'd scared herself a few times, imagining that she heard the huge trunk lid creaking open, with a skeletal hand coming forth; and that the headless sewing dummy had moved several feet closer to her. But that was impossible.

Now that it was raining, the attic was more mysterious than ever. With the roof directly above her, Susan could hear only the rain beating against the tiles. And with no sunlight coming through the attic's lone window, the room looked as if an early dusk had fallen.

She saw all this as she stood at the top of the stairs surveying the assorted boxes, trunks, sacks, and stacks of old magazines. That was how the attic smelled—mildewy—the sour way old magazines smell when they've been left in a dank basement.

There was only one thing Susan didn't expect to see and that was her grandfather standing at the attic window. She'd never seen Gramps up here before. She wondered why he was here.

He stood at the window, looking out. His back was to her. He said, "Go downstairs and wait for me, Susan."

His voice startled her. He didn't sound like Gramps at all. The voice was too deep and too cold.

"Do you hear me, Susan?"

"But, Gramps—"

"Do as I say!"

Sharp as his voice was, he didn't turn around to face her.

She looked at the worn blue cardigan sweater with the line of white shirt riding above it; the gray, wrinkled work pants; and the old flannel house slippers he liked so much . . . the slippers that she heard slap-slap-slapping down the hall at night when he was on the way to his room.

Susan sometimes thought that she loved Gramps even more than she loved Mom and Dad.

Until the last couple of weeks, anyway. Gramps had changed somehow. He wasn't . . . Gramps. Not exactly, at any rate.

"Can't I just come over and say hi?" Susan said.

"No. Get out of here."

Gramps was no longer just impatient. Now he was angry.

"But, Gramps—"

And then, before even she was aware of what she was doing, she stepped across the shadowy room to the tall, old figure of Gramps and touched her hand to his.

And immediately let out a cry of pain.

Gramps's flesh had been searing to touch.

But that wasn't all. She'd glimpsed his face . . . a face that did not belong to her beloved Gramps.

This face was so deeply lined it looked like a mask, and its eyes were a glowing azure color, and its mouth was filled with some kind of frothing green fluid.

She'd seen all this in a single glimpse.

"Gramps. Can I talk to you?"

"I don't want to hurt you, Susan. Get out now while you still can."

She started to take a step toward him and then remembered how hot his hand had been. And how grotesque his face had been.

This was not Gramps.

She didn't run. She didn't even walk quickly.

She simply turned around and very slowly—and very sadly—walked down the attic steps to the second floor.

She went into her bedroom and threw herself on the bed and buried her face in her hands. And she stayed that way—thinking of the old man upstairs who was somehow not her Gramps—until she drifted off to sleep.

She had a terrible dream. She was climbing a tall bell tower. Up, up, up she went on the winding, dark staircase. She was afraid of what awaited her—yet she seemed compelled to go on from here.

She reached the top step and paused. She looked deep into the darkness, to where the huge bell hung inside the belfry.

And then a man stepped forward from the shadows—

A man with skin as old and wrinkled as a corpse that had lain for decades underground—

And then she was screaming, screaming as the ancient man stepped toward her—

She woke to a pounding on the door. "Are you all right, Susan?"

Sweating, not sure where she was, Susan glanced around her room. Everything looked unfamiliar.

Her mother opened the door and peeked in. "Bad dream, honey?"

Her mother's face brought it all back—her house, her room, her bed—

And Gramps.

Her mother came over and sat down on the bed with her. Outside the rain continued to fall, cold and silver in the early dusk. Wind scraped naked November branches against the window.

Susan wrapped her arms around her mother's waist and hugged her.

"He isn't Gramps anymore."

"Who isn't Gramps anymore?"

"Gramps isn't."

Her mother held Susan away and looked at her

carefully. "Is that what your dream was about—Gramps?"

"Yes."

"And in the dream he wasn't Gramps?"

"He was a monster. His eyes were real strange and his skin was hot when you touched it—just the way it was in the attic."

Susan's mother smiled. "I told you going up there would give you bad dreams. The attic even scares me a little bit."

"But, Mom, please listen to me. He isn't Gramps anymore."

"Then who is he, honey?"

"He's a . . . monster. That's what I'm trying to tell you."

Susan wrapped herself around her mother's waist again. "I know you don't believe me."

"Honey, I believe that you may believe that Gramps has turned into a monster. But if he had, don't you think I'd know it? After all, I've been his daughter for thirty-four years."

Susan started to say something more, but before she could get the words out, her mother said, "Now you go wash for dinner. We're having chicken dumplings and chocolate pie. And then afterwards, you can listen to your programs on the radio."

Chicken dumplings. Chocolate pie. Radio programs. What little girl could possibly resist the prospect of all that?

"Feel better?" her mother said, hugging her.

"Yes," Susan said. And she did. When she thought about it now—after talking to her mother—she was sure he was wrong.

How could lovable old Gramps have become a monster?

Susan's father was a prominent insurance executive and a man who made no secret of the fact that he was extremely lucky. Three years earlier, he had been a soldier in the Pacific theater. One night, during a Japanese air attack, he had been wounded so badly that the doctors had given up on him.

Indeed, his condition had been so critical that the doctors decided not to operate on him. They saw no point. He wouldn't live, and there were other wounded men whom surgery might help.

Somehow, miraculously, he woke up just at dawn and called out for help. He had not only regained consciousness, he had also regained amazing strength.

At dinner tonight, the handsome, tow-haired man in the brown tweed suit looked as if he'd never been sick in his life.

Tim Daily led the family in saying grace and then started passing the food around to his daughter, Susan, his son, Rich, his wife, Marcia, and her father, George.

Both children ate quickly, not wanting to miss "The Lone Ranger," which was their favorite radio show. After that would come an evening with such radio stars as Jack Benny and Bob Hope and an eerie adventure in the land of "Inner Sanctum."

Conversation at the table was typical. Tim Sr., talked about the economy—how a lot of ex-GIs couldn't find jobs because of the recession. Marcia talked about a big sale starting tomorrow at a downtown department store. Susan and her brother chattered on about events at school. And Gramps—

Gramps was curiously silent.

Ordinarily, George enjoyed regaling the family with tales of the "old days" as he invariably called them . . . big-time sports figures he'd known, and his time in Europe during World War I.

But something was different tonight.

For one thing, he hadn't touched a bit of his food.

For another, he had shown no interest in any of the conversation.

All he did was sit and stare at his plate. And then raise his head and look carefully at each person at the table, as if they were somehow strangers to him.

And say nothing—not a single word.

"Are you feeling all right, Dad?" Marcia asked.

Gramps turned his head slowly and looked at her. His blue eyes were curiously empty of emotion.

"Yes," he said.

Susan wondered if anybody else noticed his voice. How strange it sounded.

"Did you work this morning, Gramps?" Tim asked. He was proud of a sixty-eight-year-old man who still wanted to work.

"Before the rain started," Gramps said in that hollow voice again.

Marcia smiled. "I suppose digging graves in the rain wouldn't be much fun."

"We're proud of you, Gramps," Tim said. "Whoever thought a man your age would find a part-time job at Windmere Cemetery?"

Susan had avoided looking at Gramps tonight, afraid he would suddenly turn into the monster he'd been in the attic. Her mother's talk had faded . . . and Susan was again convinced that Gramps was no longer himself.

Now she felt his eyes on her. She raised her own gaze and met his.

She thought she saw, deep down in the pupils of his blue eyes, the azure glow she'd seen earlier in the day.

Gramps stood up suddenly.

"Excuse me. I think I'll take a rest."

Marcia and Tim, Sr., exchanged troubled glances. What was wrong with Gramps?

Marcia started thinking about an article she'd read recently . . . one that noted a "flulike" state that preceded certain kinds of heart attacks.

"Maybe I'd better go check on him," she said.

Tim nodded.

A few minutes later, he led his two children into the living room. They got comfortable in the easy chairs set in front of the big Philco radio while Dad got the proper station in tune.

Susan kept thinking about the monster that she suspected had taken over Gramps—

Or she did for a time, anyway.

But when the stirring trumpet sound announcing the Lone Ranger came through the radio speaker—accompanied by the even more stirring sounds of a galloping horse named Silver—she forgot all about Gramps and got caught up in tonight's adventure.

Two days later, her mother out shopping, her brother down the block playing with friends, Susan came into the house.

She went about the usual business of hanging her coat up in the downstairs closet, making herself a snack of an oatmeal cookie and a small glass of milk, and going upstairs and changing into her corduroy pants and her sweatshirt with Superman on the front of it. She'd ha her mom send in money, along with a box top from Pep, which was Susan's favorite cereal.

She took her Nancy Drew book into the den downstairs, turned on the light, opened to Chapter Eight and started reading. Nancy and George were creeping into this abandoned house. The scene was really scary. Just then wind rattled the windows and Susan shivered.

She read for twenty minutes and then put the book down. Something wasn't right in the house. Then she realized that she hadn't seen or heard Gramps. He frequently took a nap about this time. She decided to go check his room, which was downstairs in the basement. Dad had gotten knotty pine and completely finished the lower level. Now it was just as nice as the rest of the house. Gramps even had his own shower and toilet down there.

She went to the head of the basement stairs and opened the door.

"Gramps?" she called.

The basement was dark. Very dark. She reached up to turn on the basement light. She clicked the switch several times. Nothing. The light must be burned out, she reasoned.

"Gramps?" she called again.

After waiting a full minute, she decided to go down the stairs.

She'd hold on to the railing and take one cautious step at a time. Gramps was probably sleeping.

She felt lonely and wanted to talk to somebody. She didn't like coming home to an empty house.

The stairs were very steep. When she'd been very little, she'd always had nightmares of tripping and falling down these steps.

She gripped the railing and started downward.

She took her time.

The closer she got to the floor, the more the smell imposed itself on her. It was a kind of sickly-sweet odor. All she could liken it to was a dead bird Dad had found on the back porch one time. The bird was all bloated and ugly in death . . . and gave off an acrid odor that made her clamp her hand over her nose and mouth and run into the kitchen.

This smell kept getting worse and worse.

She put a foot down and touched the basement floor. Total darkness. To the left she could make out the hulking shape of the Lennox furnace. To the right she could see the vague shape of Gramps's metal shower stall and his little nook of a room pushed over in one corner—single bed, clothesline for hanging his clothes, and bookcase with his beloved collection of Zane Grey westerns.

"Gramps?"

And then she heard it for the first time, a sound of very nasal, and very troubled, breathing.

Gramps.

It had to be.

"Gramps?" she said again.

When she got no answer, she decided to walk through the very deep darkness over to his bed.

She tried not to think about the monster she'd seen in the attic the other day. She had to have imagined that. . . . Had to. Gramps becoming a monster wasn't real. It was just the kind of thing adults told little kids to scare them.

By the time Susan reached the single bed, the smell was so bad that her eyes were running with tears and she felt sure she was going to throw up.

All she could see was darkness.

All she could hear was the raspy breathing of the dark figure on the dark bed.

"Gramps?"

She felt as if she were walking on the bottom of a very black ocean.

"Gramps?"

Her knees touched his bed.

The rasping was now very loud.

The odor was overpowering.

"Gramps?"

And then in the dark, just as she was able to make out the shape of her grandfather lying on the bed, two eyes snapped open, and she found herself staring into the same inhuman azure glow she'd seen in the attic.

She screamed.

Gramps started to sit up on the bed. Green juices ran from his mouth. In the light from his eyes she could see that the skin was rotted and torn.

He clamped his hand on her wrist.

She screamed again and tried to wrench herself free.

And then she realized that her flesh was burning where his fingers held her.

He started up from the bed and said, "You would not listen, Susan. And now you must join me."

The voice was as it had been in the attic—distant, cold, dead in some way.

Not knowing what else to do, she kicked him in the shins. She would have felt terrible about this if this had really been Gramps . . . but it was not Gramps . . . it was somebody . . . something . . . else.

The kick had the desired effect.

Whatever Gramps had become, the kick had hurt him. He eased his grip on her frail wrist.

She took off running, stumbling over a hassock and

tripping but picking herself up again and running toward the dim shape of the stairway.

Gramps was not far behind her.

"Come here, Susan. Come here at once."

She grabbed the railing.

Started climbing.

Once, she tripped and banged her knee so hard it bled.

But she didn't dare stop.

She had to keep climbing . . . climbing.

"Please come here, Susan. Please come here."

Had . . .to . . . reach . . . the . . . kitchen . . . the . . . side . . . door . . . escape.

She looked back down the stairs only once . . . and saw Gramps . . . eyes eerily aglow . . . beckoning to her with a skeletal hand.

Then she saw him put one foot on the stairs.

He was coming up after her.

She had to hurry . . . had to.

Susan waited out by the garage until her mother came home in the nice, new DeSoto Dad had bought her last fall.

As soon as she saw her mother, Susan ran to her and wrapped her arms around her and, in between sobs, told her everything that had happened.

Marcia left the groceries in the car and told Susan to wait outside. Marcia was going inside and find out what was going on.

When her mother didn't return in ten minutes, Susan got frightened. Had Gramps attacked his own daughter?

An ear-splitting siren worked its way toward Susan's house and before she knew what was going on, she saw the boxy white emergency vehicle pull up in front of her house. Two white-uniformed men promptly ran out of the car. One of them was carrying a portable stretcher. They ran straight up the stairs to the front door. Marcia let them in. Susan ran around front for a better look at everything.

A lot of the neighbors came to watch, standing on their lawns or the sidewalk, a few of them obviously offering up prayers that everything would work out all right.

A few minutes later, Gramps was carefully carried from the house to the ambulance on the stretcher.

Susan was afraid to look at him as he went past. She didn't ever want to see that monstrous face again.

But as the attendants came abreast of her, Susan couldn't help herself. She opened her eyes and took her last look at Gramps.

He looked fine. Like regular old Gramps. Kindly. Patient. Loving. And now he looked very sad, too. His blue eyes were open, but you could see that he was confused and afraid. He was dying and he didn't quite know what to make of it.

In time the ambulance left, and the neighbors went home, and Marcia raced to the hospital to be with her father.

Around nine that night, Gramps died.

Three days later, there was a funeral. Susan saw lots of aunts and uncles and cousins she hadn't seen in a long time. There was a funeral mass and then prayers said at the very chilly graveside and then ham sandwiches and cake and pie and milk and Pepsi at home for all the relatives. Susan ate more than her share.

Susan never again mentioned the two incidents with Gramps to her mother. She knew instinctively that it would just upset Marcia . . . and subtly turn her against Susan. Marcia had obviously not believed Susan's story. . . .

By the time Marcia had found her father in the basement, he had somehow become plain old Gramps again.

And that was how Marcia wanted to remember her father forever. As lovable old Gramps, not a monster.

Lorraine Warren

No other tenet of the paranormal is scoffed at quite so readily as demonism—when a human being is changed into something monstrous.

Even people who believe in paranormal activity express doubts about such a transformation.

Dr. A. K. Reinhardt, for instance, noted that "Demonism is invariably transference—person A begins to sense some personality change in person B and thus begins to imagine that B has also begun to change physically, symbolic of the inner or spiritual shift. . . ."

Reinhardt goes on to argue that many people report physical changes in their spouses—after their spouses have said that they want out of the relationship.

Reinhardt cites as evidence of this a New Hampshire case in which a husband bludgeoned his wife to death with a hammer and explained to the court psychiatrist that "she had turned into a monster and planned to hurt our children."

But given the number of "demonic" reports we've had over the years, and the number of similar incidents reported by other groups studying psychic activities, we simply don't believe that all these examples of demonism are imaginary.

Dr. Reinhardt is a serious psychic investigator, but we think he needs to look again at this subject.

A Friendly Spirit

IN 1968 Mary Rogers was a housewife with two children in preschool and a husband in Vietnam. Her husband's military salary was enough so that Mary was not forced to take a job outside her home.

There was one problem with rarely going anywhere . . . Mary, ordinarily a slender, attractive woman, found that her body was ballooning. She'd gotten into watching soap operas and snacking while she did so. And without a husband to look good for, Mary soon found herself with twenty added pounds.

One sunny morning she stood in front of her mirror, disgusted with what she saw. Her husband's tour of duty would end in seven months . . . and then she'd have to crash off the weight.

Why not start on a sensible diet now, rather than waiting till the last moment?

Mary continued to fix the meals her two girls liked—

ham and pork chops and hamburgers—but she cut all her own portions in half.

Mary also began jogging five mornings a week.

Her route took her up through some steep hills . . . and down past Del Mar Cemetery.

One morning, as she jogged past, Mary heard a strange voice in her mind. It wasn't her own voice . . . that was for sure.

The voice was female and older.

It seemed to be speaking from far away.

Mary glanced around. Where was the voice coming from?

Finally the voice and its whispery words faded away . . . and Mary forgot all about it.

Two mornings later, jogging in the same area, the voice returned . . . this time stronger and more distinct than it had been before.

As Mary continued to move past the cemetery, the voice began to speak directly to her.

—My name is Helen. I want to be your friend, Mary. I want to help you through some troubled times ahead.

Mary felt real panic. Was she losing her mind? Her family had a history of mental illness. Was such an illness now overtaking her?

The voice was silent for the rest of her run.

That night, the girls in bed, Mary sat up very late watching Johnny Carson and thinking about the voice she'd heard that morning.

What had the voice meant, "I want to help you through some troubled times."

What troubled times?

Despite the fact that her husband was off fighting a war, Mary's life would be envied by many other, less fortunate women.

And then, very late, the phone rang.

She jumped, startled, when she heard it.

And then a terrible feeling started up from her
stomach and spread into her chest.

Bad news. Nobody called this late at night unless it
was bad news.

And that likely meant her husband in Vietnam.

"Hello."

"Mary Rogers?"

"Yes."

"I'm a friend of your husband's. Mike Harcourt."

"Oh?"

"I'm sorry for calling so late but . . . well, our
'copter crashed tonight, and I thought I'd call you
before the army did. I'm just outside of Saigon."

"Is he . . . ?"

There was a pause. "I couldn't find him. We went
down in rain and fog. There wasn't any gunfire. The
'copter just developed some kind of mechanical problem and all of a sudden we lost control." Another pause.
"I walked away fine but I couldn't find Don. The only
possibility is—"

"Yes?"

"That he was captured. That there were some Cong
in the underbrush around where we crashed, and they
somehow . . . got hold of him." Pause. "I just wanted
to tell you that earlier tonight he was showing everybody those photos you took of yourself and the girls at
the science museum. He was really proud."

Mary began to weep.

"He may be fine, Mary. He may just be . . . lost."

But Mary knew better. All these months she had
practiced what her father always called "whistling pa-

the graveyard"—not allowing herself to think that anything could happen to Don over in Vietnam.

Somehow he would be . . . fine.

But tonight's phone call had changed everything.

"The captain's sending a patrol out to look for him, Mary. I'll keep you posted. Don, he's—he's my best friend, and this is the least I can do." Now Mike Harcourt sounded as if he wanted to cry.

Mary thanked him and quietly hung up. She did not sleep the rest of the night.

The army called the following day and said that Don was being listed as MIA, Missing In Action. Mary listened in weary disbelief to all the hopeful words uttered by the military man on the other end of the phone—but she did not share his optimism. It was clear to her that her husband was dead.

Mary called Don's folks. Naturally they became upset. They said they'd drive down and be with her but Mary said that, for now anyway, until they knew something further, she'd rather be alone with her two daughters. She hoped she didn't offend them but she simply did not want company at such a stressful time.

Mary took a sleeping pill that night. She slept peacefully, and when she woke up, she felt filled with energy—despite the depression and anxiety that gnawed away at her.

But she wouldn't be much use to the girls if all she did was sit around and brood.

She asked a neighbor to come over and watch the girls while she went jogging. She felt that exercise would buoy her spirits and clear her mind.

She took her usual path, the lovely countryside

around Denston very green on this bright spring morning.

As she approached the cemetery, she thought again of the voice she'd heard the other day . . . the voice warning her about "some troubled times."

She almost turned around and ran back the other way.

She felt she would absolutely fall apart if she heard that voice today—

But she didn't fall apart at all.

Indeed, when the voice came to her, it sounded as warm and reassuring as an old friend.

—He's not dead, Mary. No matter what the army says . . . or no matter what you might fear, your husband is alive.

Mary realized then that the voice somehow came from the cemetery. She stopped and walked over to the gravestones on the sloping hill. And stood there. And gave herself over completely to the experience.

Who are you? Mary asked.

—My name is Helen. I was born in 1868 and I died in 1903. The Divine Spirit often uses me to comfort people.

You said my husband is not dead?

—Soon you'll know the truth, Mary.

And then Helen's *presence* left Mary . . . who now stood very alone in the cemetery . . . suddenly aware of the birds and the sounds of distant traffic.

Should she believe what the spirit had told her?

She began jogging again.

Her course usually took her three miles but today she ran six—and was hardly aware of it—she was so preoccupied with Helen's words.

Was Don really alive?

After she got home and took a shower and fixed

lunch for the girls, Mary picked up the phone and started to call Don's mother to tell her about Helen.

But then she stopped herself.

Ida, Don's mother, would just think Mary was being silly. While Don's parents weren't outright atheists, they were at least agnostics. Mary, a reasonably faithful Episcopalian, had frequently argued with Don about how the girls should be raised. Finally Don had relented and had let Mary start taking the girls to church each Sunday.

Mary put down the phone.

No, if she told Ida that she'd been talking with a spirit, Ida might even try to have the girls taken away from her . . . saying that the grief of Don's disappearance had made her mentally ill.

Three more days passed.

Each morning Mary got up and jogged but she had no contact with Helen.

She wondered if she'd done something to offend the woman. Perhaps Mary hadn't seemed grateful enough for Helen's reassurances.

On the fourth day Helen returned.

This time Mary had not quite reached the graveyard when Helen's voice sounded in her head.

—They will find your husband today. And he will be safe, though he will be in the hospital for some time.

Mary angled into the cemetery and walked among the gravestones. Somehow Helen's voice always seemed stronger when Mary was here, walking over the dewy grass and filling herself with the sense of history this place gave her.

—You must be strong, Mary, and you must keep faith.

Mary nodded.

—Sometimes God tests us. And this may be a test for you . . . to be strong no matter how people may treat you.

And then the voice went away.

Mary completed her jogging and went home.

She was just about to step into the shower when the phone rang.

Her father-in-law, Donald, Sr., said, "Mary, I wondered if you'd talk to Ida. She's having a very bad day. She was up all night thinking about Don."

"Of course, put her on."

Ida got on the phone and said, "I'm sorry I'm not handling this better, Mary. I keep trying to find strength in myself but—"

Mary could tell that Ida was embarrassed for the way she was acting.

But the prospect of losing a son was something that would make most mothers crumble.

Especially mothers who had no religious faith to draw strength from.

"I'm going to tell you something, Ida," Mary said.

"Tell me something?"

"I know it will sound crazy but it isn't. It really happened."

Now Ida's voice changed from one of soft pain to hard apprehension. "What will sound crazy, dear?"

"I've been in touch with a spirit, and she's assured me that Don is all right. He isn't dead."

Long silence on the other end of the phone.

"Dear, would you like Donald, Sr., to come over there?"

Mary had to laugh.

"No, Ida, I'm fine. Really. I just want you to feel as
onfident about your son as I do."

"You've been in touch with a spirit, you say?"

"Yes."

"Perhaps I'd better put Donald, Sr., on, dear."

Which is just what she did.

"Are you all right, Mary?" Donald, Sr., wanted to
now. "What the hell did she mean about a 'spirit,'
nyway?"

So Mary told him.

And almost immediately wished she hadn't.

"You know how we feel about religion," Donald,
r., said. He was a college math teacher. He believed
nly in what he could see, feel, smell—which was a
urious attitude, Mary had long thought, for somebody
ho worked daily with the numbers . . . which were
least as abstract as spirits and goblins and demons.

"I was just trying to make her feel better. The spirit
ld me that Don would be found today."

"Today, eh?" Donald, Sr., said skeptically. "Well,
t's hope that 'spirit' of yours is right."

"I'm sorry if I upset her."

Mary heard whispering on the other end of the
one. "Mary, Ida thinks it would be a good idea if
e'd come and stay with you and the girls."

"I'd really rather be alone."

"She just wants to be sure—"

"—sure that I'm not crazy, and that I won't harm the
rls, and that I won't perform any satanic rituals here."
ue regretted her sarcasm at once. These were decent
ople. "I'm fine, Donald. Reassure Ida of that. I'm fine
d so are the girls."

He sighed. Spoke softly. "Ida's out of the room now,

Mary. Just please don't talk about spirits or anything like that to her again, all right?"

"All right."

"It upsets her—even though I know you were just trying to help."

Around two o'clock that afternoon the rain started. Mary stood at the window watching silver beads run down the glass. She felt like a small child who had to stay in and color and play with dolls because her mother wouldn't let her play in the rain.

She tried reading a mystery but gave up after a few pages. She tried watching TV but the soap opera actor seemed wooden and almost comic.

The phone rang.

A man identified himself as an army officer and gave her the news. "Your husband has been found eighteen miles east of Saigon. Apparently the crash caused him shock, and shock caused him amnesia. He was wandering around in the jungle, and I have to tell you, it's a miracle he survived. The particular area is crawling with enemy. He still hasn't recovered his memory, but the medical people tell me that this is a temporary state. He's undergoing the last part of his physical exam right now. We'll have him call you in a few hours. When you're talking to him, just keep in mind that right now he's not in the best of condition mentally but that he'll soon be fine."

After hanging up, Mary offered a prayer of thanks and then dialed Ida's number right away.

"He's alive and well except for some amnesia, Ida."

Ida shouted for Donald, Sr., to pick up the extension in the living room.

"Hello?"

"He's alive and well, Donald," Mary said, and then went into the explanation the military man had given her.

"So the amnesia is temporary?" Donald, Sr., asked.

"That's what he said."

"I feel like—celebrating," Ida said. "Why don't we drive down and take you and the girls out for a nice dinner somewhere?"

Mary smiled. "That sounds great, Ida. And by then I'll be able to tell you what Don said when he called."

Pause.

Ida: "I'm sorry if I hurt your feelings, Mary."

"You didn't. That's fine."

Donald: "I guess your 'spirit' was right, after all."

Even though he was gently mocking her, Mary said: "I guess I have my beliefs and you have yours."

"Well, we certainly didn't mean to imply that you were—"

"I understand," Mary said. "And it's fine."

A few hours later, Don called. The conversation was stiff at first, but after a few minutes he loosened up and even made a joke about his condition. "I'm looking at a photograph of you and the two girls. I'm sure a lucky guy—whoever I am."

"The doctor said you'll have your memory back in a very short time."

"Will I find out I'm a millionaire?"

"No, but you'll find that you have five people who sure love you a whole lot. Me and the girls and your parents."

Sixty days later, Don came home to the States. By then his memory was back.

He found a job managing an office equipment store. He and Mary renewed their marriage vows.

In the spring of 1976, still curious about the voice of Helen, Mary told her story to a friend who had recently gone to hear the Warrens lecture. The friend told Mary that she should contact the Warrens, which, after a week of hesitation, she did.

Ed Warren

Most people fear ghosts and with good reason. Down through the centuries, ghosts have been portrayed as evil beings bent on terrifying and, in some cases, even destroying humanity.

In a very good article entitled "Our Friends the Ghosts," Dr. Wylie Beaufort posits a very different notion.

"In fact, in investigating the activities of ghosts for the past thirty years," Beaufort writes, "I've learned that ghosts frequently try to help the human beings with whom they come in contact.

"In most instances, ghosts seem to be lonely or troubled souls who for one reason or another have not been properly assimilated into the spirit world. They seem possessed of modest extrahuman powers . . . especially precognition.

"Many ghosts have the ability to warn their human friends of impending trouble, or even to bring messages from the spirit world.

"I've personally met three ghosts who turned out to be very friendly spirits indeed."

One thing we've learned, Lorraine and I, is that when

you become seriously involved in psychic investigation, you find yourself reaping many rewards.

We feel certain that there's life beyond this one, and we know that we will someday see again those who have gone on before us.

Our lives are exciting, ever-changing, and rich with proof of God's place in the vast universe . . . in all its realms.

Ghost Stalker

IN HIS way, Henry Wayne Suter was precocious. At age five, he trapped a robin in a small cage and then proceeded to cut off its wings with his father's hunting knife. At age six, he took a neighbor's puppy, squirted liquid lighter fluid all over it and set it on fire. He later explained to his mother that the puppy made "funny sounds" when it was on fire, sounds young Henry liked to hear.

Then, at age nine, there was the matter of the seven-year-old neighbor girl whom Henry tied up in his garage. He stripped her of her clothes, began to poke and prod all her private parts with a stick, and then began to whip her with his belt. Even though she was gagged and her screams could not be heard, he liked the wet dark fear he saw in her eyes. Fortunately for the girl, Henry's mother happened to be hanging laundry on the clothesline later in the afternoon. Having heard a kind of whimpering sound, she peeked in the window and saw the girl.

Now you might imagine that Henry was the class weirdo or freak, one of those strange, chubby, silent boys who always turn up twenty years later on the late news for going into their former place of employment and blowing away six or seven of their former co-workers.

On the contrary—Henry was possessed of curly golden locks, bright and brazen blue eyes, a shiny Hollywood smile, and enough social skills to make him class president six years running. While not a gifted athlete, he was good enough to make both the basket-ball and football teams; and while not a great singer, he invariably had at least one solo in every glee club musical at the Erie, Pennsylvania, high school he attended in the late eighties.

By boys, he was much sought after as a friend; by girls, given his looks, he was hotly pursued as a date.

Henry was fourteen when he killed his first human.

It happened this way: Henry's father, a salesman for a prosperous pharmaceutical company, felt that Henry was now old enough to hold a summer job. He sent Henry down to the unemployment office, where a woman told him that she could get him a job unloading trucks at a local beer distributor's. The job was simply to stack up the empty cases, which would eventually be taken inside the bottling plant, where the bottles would be washed in scalding water.

Henry enjoyed physical labor. He liked the feel of his muscular body running with sweat. Liked the exhaustion that followed a hard day's work. He was happy to take the job.

Six days into his duties, however, Henry started to have second thoughts. Looking out the window from the warehouse where he toiled off-loading empty cases of beer from big trucks, Henry saw pretty girls riding their bicycles in the hot, bright summer sun. He wanted to be with those pretty girls. He did not want to be stuck inside where everything smelled of truck exhaust and stale beer.

One of Henry's co-workers was a Mexican-American named Juarez, a fifty-year-old man who'd taken a quick dislike to the yellow-haired and tirelessly arrogant Henry. Juarez was technically Henry's boss, even though both of them took most of their orders from the big boss, Windom. Juarez constantly told Henry that he was not working quickly enough or skillfully enough.

"In the time you can unload six cases, I can unload twice as many. And look at those stacks of yours. They're uneven. They'll fall down. You wait and see." Juarez pretty much kept this up eight hours a day.

One day Henry saw Juarez up on the catwalk. Juarez liked to stand up there, many many feet above the concrete floor, and smoke a cigarette.

On this day Henry joined him, lighting up one of his own cigarettes and leaning his elbows on the catwalk.

"How far down you think it is?"

"Long, long way, kid."

"Twenty feet?"

"More than that."

"Thirty?"

"Maybe forty, kid."

Henry smoked some more and stared down at the floor. "You think it'd kill you?"

"Do I think what would kill you?"

"Falling from up here."

"Are you crazy? It sure as hell would kill you."

"That's what I figured."

Two days later, Henry again saw Juarez up on the catwalk. Again Henry joined him.

"I bet your head would bust open like a melon. If you fell from here, I mean."

"It sure would, kid. It sure would."

And as if to illustrate this, Juarez flipped his cigarette out into space and then watched the white butt fall to the floor below.

On impact the lighted end of the cigarette exploded into a dozen fiery fragments.

Juarez looked at Henry and smiled. "Just like that, kid. Just like that."

Juarez turned and started to lead the way around the catwalk. When he was finished with his break, he expected you to be finished, too, even if you'd started ten minutes later than he had.

Henry looked around.

On a lazy summer afternoon the big shadowy warehouse was empty. At the moment there weren't even any trucks backed up to the dock for unloading.

The time was perfect. And so were the circumstances. He knew he had to move quickly. And he did.

Juarez was a small, burly man, and when Henry first lifted him, he wondered if he'd have strength enough to raise him over the catwalk guardrail and throw him to the floor below.

Juarez screamed obscenities all the way down.

When his head struck the floor, there was a loud popping noise.

Juarez's dark eyes remained open, but all life died in them.

Then blood began streaming from the rear of his skull.

Henry started yelling for help. He knew he needed to sound scared and sad.

After all, as he said at the funeral to Mrs. Juarez, "Your husband was my best friend, ma'am. I had a lot of respect for him."

No questions were ever asked about the death. Purely accidental. As usual, Juarez had had alcohol in his system, and in some freak way he'd stumbled and pitched head first from the catwalk.

Poor Henry had done everything he could do to save him.

Over the next few years, Henry developed new interests such as chopping up dogs, cats, and even a large milk snake, which he cut up into sections with a meat clever. He was fascinated with the way each section of the snake stayed animated even after being cut off.

And he found himself a new hobby.

In the late 1960s, which was when Henry was loose to prey upon civilization, hitchhiking was a fashionable means of transportation.

In the fifties there had been several grisly hitchhiker murders. Pick up the wrong person on the wrong rainy night . . . and you might find yourself, as one California man had, with your eyeballs cut out, your arms chopped off, and your sex lying next to your corpse on the bloody seat.

But with the coming of hippies and free love and the real or imagined commitment to "brotherhood," hitchhiking came back into fashion.

Henry loved to get into the nice new Firebird his father had bought him for his sixteenth birthday and scare the hell out of hitchhikers.

It worked this way: he'd pick up a hitchhiker, preferably female and preferably cute, and then be sure to drive past Harcourt Cemetery—but beforehand he'd soften them up with horrifying tales of a dead man named "Don," who, during his days as a human being, used to walk the land killing young women. Henry would describe in graphic detail what "Don" did to his victims.

By the time they reached the cemetery, the hitchhikers were usually spooked by Henry's tales.

Then Henry would pretend that his car stalled, leaving them alone on the road running past the cemetery.

"Guess I'd better see what's wrong with the engine," Henry would say.

And then get out of the car.

And go around front and lift up the hood.

And then vanish.

Henry always pulled his car so far off the road that he could easily crawl away from the vehicle when the hood was up and hide behind a tombstone.

Put yourself in the girl's place. You're hitchhiking across country. You're in a strange place and very tired. And all of a sudden the handsome young man driving the car goes up to see why the engine suddenly stalled.

And then he vanishes.

You sit there and call out for him, but there's no answer.

And then you realize how dark it is.

How few cars are passing by.

And you look over at the graveyard, the headstones ghostly in the pale moonlight.

And much as you don't want to, you start thinking about "Don," the psychopathic killer Henry had been telling you about.

What if the spirit of "Don" really did prowl the cemetery at night, as Henry insisted?

And what if his appetite for young women needed to be sated once again?

So dark sitting here—

So lonely sitting here—

So creepy sitting here—

And then from nowhere, you see somebody jump up from the darkness on your side of the car—

A man with a hideous face—

And a long butcher knife—

And you start screaming and screaming and screaming.

At this point, even Henry found it difficult to be sadistic any longer.

He would tear off the mask and reveal himself.

It was a great trick, and it worked just the way he wanted it to until one night. . . .

Henry was sure that this particular hitcher couldn't be more than fourteen or fifteen. She lied, of course, telling him that she was eighteen. But he seriously doubted that. . . .

He picked her up one chill autumn Friday night when nearly everybody else was at one of the town football games.

She toted a backpack. Even in a P-coat and baggy jeans and a woolen cap, the girl was beautiful. No amount of disguise could hide that fact.

Henry found himself in some way smitten with her.

He couldn't stop staring at her after she got in the car.

"Where you headed?" he asked.

"Anywhere."

"Where you from?"

"Around."

"That covers a lot of territory."

She looked at him. "Chicago, if it really matters."

She made him nervous. She also made him afraid. He resented the disapproval he saw in her eyes.

"You believe in ghosts?" he said.

"No. Do you?"

"I'm not sure. But I do know that there's one around here. Supposedly, anyway."

"Could you turn up the radio a little. I like that song."

She was going to be very difficult to suck into his little game.

Bitch, he thought.

He had to wait till the song was finished to start talking about "Don" again.

"They executed him?" the girl asked.

"Uh-huh. But he came back. That's what I'm told anyway."

"That sounds like a crock."

"Coming back, you mean?"

"Yeah."

"It doesn't scare you?"

"Huh-uh. I can take care of myself."

In some curious way, he knew she wasn't kidding. She was no more than five feet one or two inches tall and weighed no more than a hundred pounds, and she was beautiful in a way that was almost frightening . . . and yet there was something hard about her, too. Something that said she had indeed been around and indeed knew how to take care of herself.

"How come you're not back in Chicago going to school?" Henry asked.

"I told you. I'm eighteen."

"Oh. Yeah. Right." He tried not to smile.

"I graduated last spring."

"Uh-huh."

Somehow the lie made her seem more vulnerable. She sounded young now and not nearly so self-confident.

He started in on the "Don" stories.

He took the long way to Harcourt Cemetery.

He wanted to get her good and worked up.

He wanted to send her running wildly, like some berserk character in a Warner Brothers cartoon, shrieking and vanishing down the long dark road.

This was going to be a lot of fun.

He reached the cemetery just after nine o'clock. Traffic was light.

He pulled over to his usual spot and said, "Damn."

"What?"

"Engine died."

"Great."

He looked at her. Her derision had started to irritate him. She sounded as if he owed her something, even though he was the one who'd picked her up.

"I'll be right back."

"Aren't you afraid?" she asked slyly.

"Afraid?"

"Yeah, I'm surprised that with big bad 'Don' prowling around out here, you'd even want to get out of the car."

"I take it you don't believe the stories, then?"

She smirked. "How dumb do I look, anyway?"

By the time he got out of the car, he was furious. The girl wasn't cooperating. She was supposed to be frightened.

Henry went through his usual routine.

He went to the front of the car, raised the hood and pretended to look inside at the motor.

He had just started to drop down and crawl across the grass to a headstone when he heard his name being called—whispered, really, and so softly that at first he felt he might be imagining things.

Who would be in the graveyard, calling out Henry's name?

Henry squinted, peering into the deep darkness of the cemetery. There was only a quarter moon tonight so there was little light.

His name was called again by the same soft and sibilant female voice.

But whose voice?

And why was it coming from the graveyard?

Henry decided to find out.

He eased himself down to his hands and knees just as he usually did. He'd check out the voice and then come back to scare the girl.

He crawled quickly into the graveyard, the grass scratchy against the palms of his hands.

And then on the far side of the cemetery he saw her, a young and voluptuous woman with flowing blond hair and a curious smile in her ice-blue eyes.

Who was she?

What did she want?

Now that he felt the girl in the car could no longer see him, Henry made his way along the perimeter of the graveyard. In moments he reached the young woman who had been calling his name.

And stopped.

Something was wrong here.

The young woman was not . . . right.

This close, he saw that she was little more than a mirage, a movie projection on the night air.

And yet she moved.

And spoke.

And came to him now.

And slid her arms around him.

And smiled at him with a face that was heartbreakingly beautiful.

And began seducing him.

And the worst thing of all was that Henry was enjoying it.

His heart pounded. His entire body became slick with sweat. He felt his groin stir resolutely.

The woman began to have sex with him right there, standing up in a corner of the graveyard.

And he was so consumed with his need that he simply gave himself up to the act—until the odors began.

All he could think of was the sourest of sewer gases.

He opened his eyes.

And just as he did so, he saw for the first time the true nature of the being that was seducing him—a crone who looked a thousand years old, with a beaky nose and hard dark eyes, and open sores on her cheeks and hands that ran with pus.

He tried to pull away from her, but at first she would not let him go.

She kept having sex with him until he finally shrank away.

She laughed at him as he stumbled backwards through the graveyard, tripping over headstones and monuments. He had never heard laughter so ghoulish or so lurid.

When he reached the car, the girl turned and looked at him and said, "Where the hell have you been? I need to get going."

He was out of breath. "There—in the graveyard—a ghost."

"Uh-huh," she said. And rolled her eyes. "A ghost."

He went around and got in on the driver's side. He laid his head against the steering wheel. He was still panting. "Didn't you hear her? You must have."

"I didn't hear anything. I just sat here waiting for you to come back."

"She was beautiful—but then she was real ugly. With sores all over her. Open sores."

The girl smirked. "Sounds like your kind of girl."

Henry was usually in control of himself. But now the girl's insolence overwhelmed him.

"Get out!" he said. "Get out!"

"You're crazy, you know that? Crazy?" And she made a little circling motion with her finger pointing to her head.

"Get out!"

Sarcastic as the girl was, she obviously saw that here was a guy having some kind of breakdown.

She didn't want to be around.

She opened the door. The overhead light went on.

For the first time she saw that some kind of slimy gelatin covered Henry's pants and shirt.

"God, what did you get into, anyway?"

"I told you, she had these sores, and they were oozing all over the place."

"Sores," she said. "Ghosts with sores. You need help, man. You need help real bad."

And with that, she got out of the car, slammed the door and set off in the direction of the highway.

Henry sat there for a long time, watching the dark graveyard for any sign of the woman who had earlier seduced him.

And then he had to look no further.

Because she was there.

Right next to him.

In the car.

She reached over, her shimmering, immaterial body radiating the same foul odor as before, and smiled up at him with her toothless mouth. "Let's go for a drive, lover. Right now."

Though he didn't want to go anywhere, the woman's command was too strong for him to resist. Somehow he had no willpower at all.

He started the car and drove back to the road.

He saw the hitchhiker standing there, smirking at him as usual.

He floored the Firebird and headed for the highway.

"I love to go fast, lover," the old crone said. "Real fast."

He noticed for the first time that she was naked, with open sores all over her body.

He hit the highway fifteen minutes later.

By then he was going seventy miles an hour.

He was afraid.

But she was in control.

"Really open her up, Henry. Really give her the gas."

"I can't go any faster."

"Sure you can, Henry. Sure you can."

And with that, she put her foot on top of his and pressed the pedal all the way to the floor.

In the meantime, she had put her hand on his sex. Despite himself, he was becoming aroused again.

The Firebird went eighty, ninety, one hundred miles an hour.

It was coming up over a hill.

Henry screamed.

He knew there was no way he would be able to stop from slamming into the back of the slow-moving semi that was ahead of him.

And there were cars in the oncoming lane. There was no way he could pass.

Henry screamed again.

And then there was just shattering glass and grinding metal and exploding gasoline.

And by now, Henry couldn't even scream any longer. Not with flames engulfing eighty percent of his body.

Lorraine Warren

Henry Wayne Suter is proof that sometimes the spirit world watches out for vulnerable people. Henry Wayne Suter was a predator—as his mother, a woman who shared her son's deathbed confession with an investigator, came to understand—and so watchful spirits took a hand in stopping him from taking any more lives.

In a study of death row inmates, Dr. H. P. Pereaux noted that "Many of these people feel that they have had supernatural experiences that drove them to do what they did. When they speak of their 'demons,' they mean this in a very literal sense."

In this case, however, a bad man was put to rest by good demons.

Epilogue

FOLLOWING OUR study of Union Cemetery, we became aware of how much our investigation had taught us. More than ever, we learned that graveyards are not "dead" at all but are "alive" with information about the supernatural and the paranormal.

This is one reason that, even today, we return again and again to Union Cemetery. There is an entire history of New England buried in its graves, a history accessible to those of enough faith and determination to find it. The video- and audiotapes we continue to make there only enhance our understanding of those realms beyond our own.

Because of our success at this cemetery, the Society is now investigating other cemeteries as well. Ghosts have been glimpsed as midnight draws near; and the dead speak clearly to the living.

No work is more vital to us these days than unlocking

the secrets of graveyards. For in the bucolic tranquillity of country cemeteries, one hears all human history in the whispers and cries and pleas of the dead.

We ask for your prayers as we continue to seek out these most profound of secrets.

—Ed and Lorraine Warren

LANDMARK BESTSELLERS FROM ST. MARTIN'S PAPERBACKS

THE SILENCE OF THE LAMBS
Thomas Harris
_____ 92458-5 $5.99 U.S./$6.99 Can.

SEPTEMBER
Rosamunde Pilcher
_____ 92480-1 $5.99 U.S./$6.99 Can.

BY WAY OF DECEPTION
Victor Ostrovsky and Claire Hoy
_____ 92614-6 $5.99 U.S.

LAZARUS
Morris West
_____ 92460-7 $5.95 U.S./$6.95 Can.

THE GULF
David Poyer
_____ 92577-8 $5.95 U.S./$6.95 Can.

MODERN WOMEN
Ruth Harris
_____ 92272-8 $5.95 U.S./$6.95 Can.

Eternal Wisdom for Today's Lifestyles

LINDA GOODMAN'S STAR SIGNS

Linda Goodman is the most respected name in astrology and metaphysics. With her usual compassion, wit, and perception, she has now written the definitive guide to putting established knowledge to work for all her readers in today's fast-paced world. It will lead you to discover your latent powers, to control your personal destiny, and to recall the forgotten harmony of the Universe.

LINDA GOODMAN'S STAR SIGNS
_____ 95191-4 $6.99 U.S./$7.99 Can.